SUPERGIRL MIXTAPES

SUPERGIRL
MIXTAPES

MEAGAN BROTHERS

HENRY HOLT AND COMPANY · NEW YORK

Henry Holt and Company, LLC
Publishers since 1866
175 Fifth Avenue
New York, New York 10010
macteenbooks.com

Henry Holt® is a registered trademark of Henry Holt and Company, LLC.

Library of Congress Cataloging-in-Publication Data
Brothers, Meagan.
Supergirl mixtapes / Meagan Brothers.—1st ed.
p.   cm.
Summary: Sixteen-year-old Maria leaves her father and grandmother in Red Hill,
South Carolina, to live with her mother, an artist, who lives with her young
boyfriend in a tiny apartment in Manhattan's Lower East Side.
ISBN 978-0-8050-8081-0
[1. Mothers and daughters—Fiction.   2. Family problems—Fiction.
3. Single-parent families—Fiction.   4. Drug abuse—Fiction.
5. Artists—Fiction.   6. Lower East Side (New York, N.Y.)—Fiction.]
I. Title.
PZ7.B79961Sup 2012   [Fic]—dc23   2011025738

First Edition—2012 / Designed by April Ward

Printed in the United States of America

1 3 5 7 9 10 8 6 4 2

for my family

And in weird shadows rhyming, plucked like lyres
The laces of my martyred shoes,
One foot against my heart.

—Arthur Rimbaud

PART
ONE

1

I'm not going back. The words pounded through my head as I sat there in Penn Station. My fists were clenched and my throat was tight. I'd been fighting off waves of queasiness for the last few hours. I didn't know where I was going, or how I was going to get there, but I knew I could not, under any circumstances, go back. Not yet.

I didn't want to prove them right. My grandmother and my dad. My grandmother never liked my mom, and whenever she wanted to needle my dad, all she had to do was bring up "that woman you married who had the nerve to abandon her own child." In my mom's defense, Dad would say, "It's more complicated than that." And, for him, that was saying a lot. He was never the type of dad to scream and yell and threaten to ground you for a month. On the other hand, we had our share of awkward silences.

Last night, when I was leaving, he finally spoke up. We were sitting in his truck, in the parking lot of the train station back home. The sun was going down. The wind blew fast-food trash across the parking lot, dead leaves skittering along behind.

"When I, um." My dad cleared his throat. "I spoke to your mother last night. She sounded excited. That you're coming to stay with her. But." He stopped. Tapping his thumb softly on the steering wheel.

"But?" I felt something sinking in my chest.

"I'm worried she won't be able to take care of you," he said.

"Dad." I rolled my eyes. "I'm almost eighteen. I can take care of myself."

"You're sixteen, and the problem is, your mother thinks she's sixteen, too."

"Then we'll take care of each other! Anyway, it's not like you're around to tuck me in at night."

I felt bad as soon as I'd said it. I'd already put my dad through a lot, and now I was leaving, maybe forever if things worked out. He stared out the window and swallowed hard, like he had a big pill stuck in his throat.

"I've been trying to help you through this, Maria," Dad said, so quietly I almost couldn't hear. "A girl needs a mother in her life. And I hope that you two get along—I really do. I just don't want to have to say 'I told you so.'"

"Why wouldn't we get along?" I asked, not expecting an answer. "She's my mom."

My dad didn't have anything else to say after that. We sat there in silence until it was time for him to load my duffel bag onto the train. Then he kissed my forehead, told me to be good, and that was that. I was gone.

I rode all night. My grandmother said it was a good way to

see the country, taking the train. I didn't ask her how much of the country I was supposed to see in the middle of the night. I called home as soon as I got to the station, but my dad was still at work. I left a message and told him everything was fine. My mom was supposed to meet the train at six a.m. Now it was almost five thirty in the afternoon. And I was still in Penn Station. Nobody was answering at her phone number. And I couldn't call my dad again. Not yet.

I had another number in my pocket. I pulled out the crumpled paper and looked at it. A page from my grandmother's day planner, printed with loops of flowering vines trailing from the corners down the page. In bright blue ink, in her looping handwriting that matched the vines, she had written a phone number and a name. *Nina Dowd.* Some old lady my grandmother knew. *Call her the moment anything happens. If you need any kind of help at all.*

She meant help with my mother. My grandmother still didn't trust her. What did she think my mom was going to do, anyway? Drop me on my head? I guess I shouldn't have been on my mom's side, considering she wasn't really around when I was growing up. I should've been angry, but I wasn't. I understood why she left. My mom was an artist. She needed to live somewhere like New York, not some podunk town like Millville, South Carolina. She needed to be around people who understood her talent, instead of people like my grandmother, who expected her to be some perfect little Southern belle. That was kind of how my grandmother wanted me to be. And I guess that's why I was on my mom's side. Even though I hadn't seen her since I was twelve, I knew how she felt. I was pretty bad at being a perfect little Southern belle, myself.

I wadded up the paper and put it back into my pocket. Forget it. I wasn't calling one of my grandmother's stick-in-the-mud friends. *One more hour,* I told myself. Then I'd check into a hotel. *Do you need credit cards for hotels?* I didn't have one. *Maybe I should call the police. No, just give her another hour.* I'd been giving her one more hour all day. *Maybe I should go look for her. Maybe something happened. She said she'd meet me in Penn Station. So keep waiting. She'll be here. I know she will.*

"Marinee-beanee!" a voice shrieked across the station. I looked up, too relieved to be embarrassed. It was her.

"Mom!"

"Look at how big you are!" She grabbed me up in a hug. The stacks of bracelets on her wrists clacked, digging into my back. It was true—I was huge. The last time I'd seen her, I was just a little shorter than she was. Now I was taller by about half a foot.

"I know. I'm a freak."

"No! It's good to be tall! You could be a model! You look amazing—they told me you were sick, so I thought—"

"I'm not sick," I corrected her quickly. "I'm fine. It was just—"

"Honey bear!" she interrupted, looking into my eyes. "Are you crying?"

"I'm just happy to see you." And I was. My mom looked the same as she always did. Thick, curly brown hair. Wide smile, serious blue eyes, heavy mascara. She was skinnier, and there were lines around her mouth now, but otherwise she looked exactly the same as she did when I was a kid.

"Your train came early! We thought we'd get here before you and buy flowers." For the first time, I noticed that my mom was part of a "we." The guy behind her was younger, dressed in a black leather jacket and jeans. His T-shirt said CHAOS THEORY and his hair stood up in glossy black spikes.

"My train came in at six."

"But it's only five thirty!" She was grabbing my bags, the usual whirlwind.

"Six a.m."

"You've been here all day?" The guy spoke. Mom was already walking ahead of us, lugging my duffel bag.

"Hey, Travis, you've got extra tokens, right?" she yelled over her shoulder.

"Yeah." He dug into his pocket and handed me a coin with a hole in the middle. We pushed through a wave of people all walking in the opposite direction until we got to a row of turnstiles.

"We'll take the A to West Fourth, then get the F to Delancey," my mother told me. I nodded as if I understood. "We're down on Rivington." I knew Rivington was the street my mother lived on, the address where I'd always sent her Christmas and birthday cards and copies of the latest stupid-looking, wallet-sized school picture.

"Come on! It's here!" I had just walked through the turnstile when my mom broke into a run. Travis caught up and took my duffel bag from her. I ran along behind, almost tripping on the graying, yellow-nubbed strip along the edge of the platform. We squeezed into the packed subway car like kids stuffing themselves into a phone booth in one of those old pictures. Everyone was dressed in fancy work clothes, suits and dresses, and gave us dirty looks over their magazines and folded newspapers as we crowded in.

"Grab a pole!" Mom warned. The train lurched forward, and I fell into a young guy in a three-piece suit carrying a leather shoulder bag and a portable CD player. He pushed me back upright without a word and adjusted his headphones. Finally, being tall was an advantage. I arched my arm over grim-faced heads to reach a long silver pole running along the top of the subway car. It felt oily, and I thought of what my grandmother had said.

"Filthy place, New York." She literally turned up her nose at lunch that day. "We will absolutely get you a pair of gloves. I wouldn't touch anything in that city, unless I wanted to catch my death."

The train shuddered and sped up, the wheels squealing. I reached higher and tightened my grip.

I'm always trying to recognize the streets, to see if I still remember. I watch the cop shows and movies they shoot in New York, and I wait for some street corner, some apartment building, to jog my memory. I was born here, but we moved when I was two. The only picture I have from that time is one of my dad holding me right after I was born. He's sitting in the windowsill of their apartment, the rusty fire escape ladder behind him. In the distance, there are rooftops and water towers. There's a tall building, fuzzy in the background, and I've asked my dad if it's the Empire State Building, but he can't remember. He says he just remembers that the apartment was downtown somewhere. I don't see how you could forget looking out your window and seeing the Empire State Building. But he says he guesses he was too busy looking after me.

I don't have any pictures of my mom from back then, but

one day, when I was around eight or nine, I was home sick from school and that movie *Desperately Seeking Susan* was on TV. I became obsessed with it, because Madonna dressed like my mom. Or maybe my mom dressed like Madonna. But I had this memory of my mom getting dressed up like that before we went out somewhere. Piling on bracelets, tying her hair back with a piece of lace. Wearing oversized Wayfarer sunglasses. Bright pink ones.

I have some memories of New York, but I'm not sure if they're things that actually happened, or if they're places I've seen on TV. I remember waking up between two bodies, my mother and father, keeping me from rolling off the bed because I didn't have a bed of my own. I remember going with my mother to a corner store that had stacks of glossy red apples outside. Those bright pink sunglasses staring down, floating above her wide smile. I remember falling down on concrete once and crying, and some strange woman stopping to pick me up. I remember my dad being upset, reaching out to take me back with his giant hands. Those same hands holding me, his voice singing me back to sleep, "Mammas Don't Let Your Babies Grow Up to Be Cowboys." I remember going over one of the bridges, standing up in the back seat of a car. The water a long way below, the city stretched out beyond, lit up in the dusk, looking like it went on forever. But they're just little flashes. My dad says he doesn't see how I could remember anything from back then. I wasn't even two.

It was right after my second birthday that we moved down to Millville. My dad had a friend who worked in a textile mill there, and he said he could get him a job as a security guard and we could live in a trailer he owned on a little piece of land by a stream. Dad said it would be warmer and cheaper, and my grandmother was only a few hours away in Atlanta and she could help take care of me. He and my grandmother had this thing about money—she wouldn't give him any, and he wouldn't ask for it. But she would buy anything I needed, because I guess she figured it wasn't my fault that my parents were always broke. Anyway, the trailer lasted two years. My mom left when I was four. She came back for a while, when I was six, but she only stayed for a few weeks. I remember her telling Dad that she wasn't cut out to be trailer trash. It was right after that that Dad bought the house near the mill where we still live, but it was too little, too late, Mom said. She filed for divorce and never came back to live with us again.

My mother had barely stopped talking since we left Penn Station. Now she was telling me about Travis's band, Chaos Theory, between mouthfuls of fries she stole from his plate. We were sitting in a booth at the Waverly Diner on Sixth Avenue. I was staring at a club sandwich I knew I couldn't eat.

"They were so freakin' good, they were just so, like, *augh*!" She made her hands into claws. "But then Jimmy and Angel wanted to move to LA—"

"And I was like, *hell* no." Travis shook his head.

"So they broke up. But Travis is putting a whole new group together, and the new bass player—what's his name? It's the name of a band, like Rush or something—"

"Slade." Travis laughed.

"Slade! Oh my gosh, he's so amazing!" She looked at her watch suddenly. "Ooh, honey, we're gonna be late." She pointed at my sandwich. "You want a to-go box for that, right?"

"Um." I looked down at my plate.

"I'll go get one." She reached into her front pockets. "I'll get some change, too."

"She's totally psyched that you're here," Travis said, sipping his Coke.

"Really?" I swallowed. "I know it all happened kind of fast."

"I think it's cool." He smiled. "It's like a little family."

I didn't know how much Mom and Travis knew. I didn't know if they knew how bad it'd gotten. How I told Dad and Grandmother that I was going to New York and I didn't care what they said. The doctor convinced them that maybe it wasn't such a bad idea. But Mom could've called my bluff. She could've said she didn't want me. But why wouldn't she want me? She always said that she couldn't afford to give me the education my grandmother wanted. That was her excuse last time I'd asked to come up and live with her in the city, back when I was thirteen and bored with Millville. This time, my grandmother said she would pay for the school herself. All my mother had to do was help me get back to normal. Whatever that was.

Mom came back to the table, slapping down singles for a tip and shoving my sandwich into a Styrofoam container at the same time.

"Okay, come on, hurry! We're running way behind!"

"What're we late for?"

"Travis and I have tickets for Lou Reed tonight. We have to take you to the apartment and then get back to the Knitting Factory."

"A knitting factory?"

"It's a club. Come on!"

And we were moving again, slinging bags and food and

shoving out through the crowd and down into the subway, toward home.

"I wish we could've gotten another ticket, but it's kind of like a secret show. Lee got an extra pair of tickets totally by chance. Oh my gosh, I can't wait for you to meet Lee! You're going to love him."

Mom finally had to stop talking to catch her breath. We were on the last of the five flights of stairs we had to walk up to get to the apartment. I didn't know how she and Travis managed to walk up all those stairs every day, but I guess I was going to have to figure it out, too.

"Okay, this is it." Mom undid two locks and the dull brown metal door of 5A swung open. I walked in, ducking beneath a strand of Christmas tree lights that was falling down from its tacked-up place over the doorway. Travis reached up and tucked the lights back above the doorjamb, and Mom flipped them on. I looked around.

"Come on, I'll give you the tour," Mom said. She pointed to a closed door. "Back there is where me and Travis sleep. The door next to that is the bathroom. This is the kitchen, obviously. And over there is your room."

"The living room?" I knew her place was small, but I thought there was more space than this. The living room was about half the size of my bedroom at home, and it was full of shelves, stacked high with books and records and videotapes. There was a TV and a couch, and a window with an air conditioner jammed into it, taped up in plastic bags for the winter.

"Don't look so worried." Mom laughed. She walked over and kicked at the couch. "It's a futon. It pulls out."

"Oh." I laughed. "Right."

"And, hey, Miss Popularity!" My mother shoved a fat manila envelope into my hands. It was decorated with foil stickers in the shape of stars. "This came for you in the mail today."

I looked at the return address. Athens, Georgia. Dory! I couldn't believe it. Dory Mason was my best friend, even though she was older than me, already in college. Her parents were my grandmother's neighbors. Dory started making me mixtapes a few years ago and sending them in the mail. I couldn't believe she'd already gotten my mom's address and sent me a new one. Especially since we'd been kind of drifting apart over the last year.

"Okay, we've gotta run, but make yourself at home. There's plenty to keep you occupied, you know, books, magazines—I've got the new *Mojo* on the table there. We don't have cable but you can watch whatever movies you want. Just put it on channel three for the VCR. Ah, I almost forgot! We left some records for you. Come here!" She grabbed my hand and tugged me over to the low shelf with the stereo, where she'd set up a display of records in a crooked march along the rug. I knelt down beside her.

"Here's our Welcome Wagon," she said, picking an album from the lineup. "Listen to this one first." She grabbed my head, her palm flat against my forehead. "It'll blow your mind."

I put Dory's package down and took the record from her. The cover was a stark, black-and-white photograph of a defiant-looking girl with a black jacket slung over her shoulder.

"Aahh! All right! Time! I know!" Mom kissed her hand and smacked it lightly against my cheek. "Don't wait up." She grabbed her keys and Travis and pulled him out the door, slamming it behind her. As soon as it was shut, it opened again.

"What am I thinking? Keep this locked, okay? And don't open it for anybody but us. Not anybody! Okay, seriously this time, we're gone. Have fun!"

And she was gone. I looked around and exhaled.

I put the record down and went to the kitchen to put my sandwich away before it got gross from sitting out. The refrigerator was wallpapered with pictures, cutouts from magazines. It was a collage of rock stars, some I recognized but most I didn't. I recognized the Beatles, with their long hair and beards. Jim Morrison in his leather pants. Bob Dylan, David Bowie, Mick Jagger with his arm around a sad-eyed blonde. I saw a picture of Kurt Cobain, the one taken of him onstage where he was standing in front of a statue and it looked like he had wings. There was one of Jeff Buckley, too, surrounded by stickers of tiny roses, right next to the one of Kurt. It made me happy, in a strange way, to see Kurt and Jeff on my mom's fridge. I loved both of them, even before they died. Now I kind of thought of them as guardian angels or something. It made me feel safer to see them there, in the kitchen in New York. I decided to give the sandwich another try.

Sometimes, when I got nervous about things, like having to give a report at school, or just worried about whatever, it was like my throat closed up and my stomach shut down and I couldn't eat anything. I'd felt like that all day long, until I saw Kurt and Jeff. I sat down at the table and started to eat. The first bite went down okay. I took another bite and sat back, chewing until it was practically liquid. I tilted my chair and looked around.

None of the four chairs around the table matched, but it

didn't matter. It wasn't even a real dining room, just a table shoved into the space where the kitchen became the living room. My room. Travis's guitars were propped up against the wall, his guitar amp next to the futon like an end table. A third guitar with no strings lay on top of the amp, along with some tools and loose strings. I guess Travis was working on it. *Travis.* Mom hadn't even mentioned that she had a boyfriend now. He was young, but he seemed okay.

I flipped through the *Mojo* magazine Mom had left on the table. It was a music magazine. The cover article was all about Keith Richards, the guitar player from the Rolling Stones. I finished off the sandwich and got up to throw the carton away. It felt better to have something in my stomach. I walked back to Mom and Travis's bedroom. There was a beaded curtain in front of the door. The beads clacked as I parted them with my hands. My mom had painted an angel on the door. I could recognize her artwork anywhere. Whenever she sent me cards, at Christmas or my birthday, she always drew them herself. She even drew little sketches on the envelopes. I saved them all in a shoebox beneath my bed. That was the whole reason she'd come to New York in the first place. To be a famous artist.

I opened the bedroom door. I guess I just wanted to see what the rest of the apartment looked like, but as soon as I went in there, I felt like I shouldn't have. The bed was unmade, and Mom's and Travis's clothes were strewn everywhere. I felt strange about seeing their clothes all together like that, and the place where they slept. Some of my mom's paintings were stacked up in the corner of the room, and I wanted to go look at them, but instead I closed the door and backed out through the beaded curtain. I peeked into the bathroom, flipping on the light. The tub was old fashioned, with claw feet. I liked that. My dad and I just had a regular, boring bathtub back home.

I looked at myself in the mirror. I looked awful. Tired and gross. My skin was pale and my forehead was broken out. My plain, long black hair was even more limp and oily than usual. There were dark circles under my eyes. I bore fangs at myself. *Grr. Ugly. Go away.*

I flipped off the light and walked back out to the kitchen. I noticed a Polaroid taped to one of the kitchen cabinets. Mom and Travis at some kind of party. She was holding the camera herself, and he was kissing her cheek. Her mouth was wide open in a surprised smile. Mom always looked like she was having a good time.

The last time I saw her, I'd just turned twelve. The phone rang late one night, and my dad picked it up. It was the weekend; he was home. I heard him pick up, and I heard him say her name. I sat up in bed, listening. She never called us—she said she couldn't afford the long-distance charges. I'd been just about to fall asleep, and I wondered if I were dreaming. But I wasn't. He kept telling her to calm down, in between long silences. Then he hung up the phone. I heard him getting up, moving around, flipping on lights. I got up and crept down the hall.

"That was Mom?"

"Yep." He was lacing up his boots.

"Is she coming back?"

"I don't know. I need to run see about her." He looked at me. I knew he was about to tell me to be good, that he'd have Mrs. Gibbs, our elderly neighbor down the street, check up on me.

"Can't I come? I haven't seen her in a really long time."

He thought about it for a while before he finally agreed. I knew how to deal with my dad. You didn't cry and scream and plead. You just stood very still and very quiet and waited for him to decide it was okay.

We drove for hours. I fell asleep, waking up once to find us parked in a Hardee's parking lot, the car doors locked and Dad on the pay phone. And waking up again when we were there. There was a sharp smell of salt and a damp chill in the air. We'd driven all the way to Myrtle Beach. The sun was coming up outside a little motel called the AquaSea Inn. We were parked beneath an arched turquoise carport. Dad took me into the motel office and told me to wait there. I went into the narrow bathroom, came back out, and settled into a well-grooved turquoise vinyl seat. The guy behind the counter swatted flies and smiled at me. He had the Weather Channel on, but he turned the dial around to a Flintstones cartoon and pushed the little TV over on the counter so that I could see it.

I licked at the bad taste inside my mouth for a few minutes, too sleepy to laugh at Fred and Barney yet, when something outside caught my eye. A heavyset man in a checked golf shirt was sort of jogging down the stairs, and sort of being pushed at the same time. The man pushing him was my dad. I saw my mom at the top of the stairs, her eyes dark, face streaked with mascara, shouting something, her mouth moving and nothing coming out. The fat man held up his hands, fumbled quickly for his keys, jerked the handle on the door of his big white car. My father kept edging up alongside him, muttering something steady and unhurried. He was barely moving, but you could tell he was winning the fight. The fat man finally got his car cranked, and he lurched out of the AquaSea parking lot. My father looked back up at my mother, his fists curled beside his pockets. She walked back into the hotel room. He began climbing the stairs.

About an hour later, Dad came and got me. By now it was the Jetsons, and the guy behind the motel counter was slumped over on his stool, snoring a little. Dad told me that Mom was in town just for the day, on business, and how would I like us all to go to breakfast together? Sure, I said. We climbed into the pickup and went to a pancake house. Mom was in a different outfit, showered and cleaned up, her mascara fresh and unsmeared. I didn't ask what her business was, and she didn't say. She acted like herself, funny and hyper, asking me about school and talking about all the places she'd take me when I came to New York. My dad didn't say much of anything, just sipped his coffee and barely ate his eggs. After the pancakes, we rolled up our pant legs and walked on the beach, running in and out of the chilly Atlantic. It was spring, before the start of the hot summer season, and there was hardly anyone else there. At one of the arcades we found a photo booth, and Mom and I made goofy faces as the camera popped. I didn't insist that my dad cram himself into the booth with us, for the same reason that I didn't ask about the man in the white car. I couldn't say what it was that kept me from insisting, except that even back then I was beginning to understand that, whatever happened between my mom and dad, they weren't getting back together again—not for their sake or mine.

Dad sliced the row of four pictures down the middle with his pocketknife and gave two to my mom, two to me. We took her to the airport that afternoon, and that was the last time I saw her in person, until today. I still had those two pictures in the shoebox under my bed at home, where I kept her letters. Now, standing in her kitchen, I looked again at the picture of Mom and Travis taped to the cabinet. She always looked so happy. I had my father's mouth. The kind of mouth that seemed to naturally turn down at the edges. I usually tried not to smile too much in pictures, anyway. My teeth were too big and crooked, even now, after two years of braces. But in those Myrtle Beach pictures, I have the stupidest grin on my face. My mom was the kind of person you couldn't help but be happy around.

I walked into the living room—my room—and sat down on the edge of the futon. My mom had left a little note card on the pillow, a sketch of a city skyline with the words "Welcome to New York" written into the windows of the buildings. I looked at the records in their procession. Knelt down in front of them again. There was Lou Reed, the guy they had gone to see. He looked like a ghost on the album cover, or maybe a little like the guy from *Rocky Horror Picture Show*. Next to it was a Ramones record—I knew a little about them from Dory. There were the New York Dolls—a bunch of guys dressed up like girls, in makeup and big bouffant hairdos! Crazy. There was a band called Television, all pale and skinny but dressed like plain, regular guys. Then there was Richard Hell and the Voidoids, with a guy in a ripped-up shirt looking coolly out of his shades, his hands on his hips. Next was a thick-lipped blond woman with her eyes turned down, looking like another ghost: Nico, *Chelsea Girl*. And the record my mom told me to listen to first. The one that was supposed to blow my mind.

I figured out how to turn the stereo on. The power light on

the record player glowed warm orange. I slid the record out of its monochrome sleeve and put it on the turntable. *Horses*, Patti Smith. I turned the volume down and put the needle on the record. There was a crackle, the needle catching the groove. I heard soft piano chords, then a woman's voice crooning. *Jesus died for somebody's sins but not mine.*

I listened for another few seconds, then I took the needle off the record. I was kind of superstitious about God stuff. My dad and I didn't go to church too often on our own—there was only one Catholic church in Millville, anyway, and it was tiny. Most people I knew went to the big First Baptist church downtown, the one that was broadcast on the local TV station, or First Methodist, the church with the best basketball team. But we went all the time when we visited my grandmother. My grandfather was Catholic, so my grandmother became Catholic, too. She was really gung ho about it, even more than my grandfather had been, according to my dad. Anyway, I hadn't been to church in a long time, but I knew it was pretty bad to say that Jesus didn't die for your sins.

My throat started tightening again. I picked up Dory's package and ripped it open along the edge. A cassette fell out. *Supergrrl Mixtape #21: Escape to New York!* And there was a note.

Hey kiddo—
Keep it real in NYC! I hope these songs treat you right.
I'm starting to get into weird girl reggae, like the Bush Tetras and the Slits. There's some live SY on here, and some Royal Trux I think you're gonna like. Also, the Rulebreaker for this installment is Urge Overkill, because

Nash Kato has the sexiest voice evah. I am going to
marry his voice someday. Butta butta butta...

Have an awesome time in NYC! Take it over, dude! And
will you CALL ME if you need me? Or just call anyway
for fun!

Love,
Dory

I couldn't help but smile. "SY" was Sonic Youth, maybe
Dory's favorite band of all time. The second or third Supergirl
Mixtape she made for me was called *Rule of Kims*, and it was
all Sonic Youth songs on one side, Breeders and Pixies on the
other. I didn't get it until she explained that the bass player for
Sonic Youth is a girl named Kim Gordon, and the bass player
for the Pixies, and the lead singer of the Breeders, is a girl
named Kim Deal. The Supergirl Mixtapes, if you haven't
guessed, are mostly girl bands, or at least bands with girl sing-
ers. But Dory always added a few Rulebreakers, which are guy
bands. "To keep it from being totally sexist," she said.

I think Dory thought of me more as a little sister than a
best friend, but that was okay by me. She was the coolest person I knew. It sucked that we hadn't been talking to each other
as much since she went to college, but she was still making me
mixtapes, at least. We could still listen to the same music and
send letters back and forth, gushing over our favorite songs. It
was as close to hanging out as we could get, especially now,
some eight hundred miles apart.

I dug my Walkman out of my backpack and put in the new
tape. The sound of snarling guitars hit my ears. I looked around

the room. There was no place to put my clothes or anything. But I didn't really care. I had made it to New York. I was finally back with my mom, back where I belonged, in the city where I was born. I sat by the window, looking out at the tops of the buildings, the lights, the cars moving along the streets, the tiny dots of people. I could see the Empire State Building in the distance, glowing white. I looked down beneath the fire escape and heard shouting, the sounds of a basketball game beneath the lights of a playground below. Horns and brakes and voices mixed with Dory's music in my headphones, and I knew that everything was getting better already.

I thought Brian was a jerk at first, then we became friends. I barely even knew him, but I saw him walking down the hall at school on the Monday after Kurt Cobain died, wearing a T-shirt beneath his Langley blazer that had Kurt's death certificate printed on it. I was so upset about Kurt that I didn't even care about being nice, or what people thought of me. I went right up to him in the hallway and said, "You're an asshole." Which was probably the worst word I'd ever said at the time. I was only thirteen.

"I am? How come?" he asked. He seemed really surprised.

"You know why." I kept walking. I was so upset. But later on, at lunch, the guy in the death certificate T-shirt found me. He sat down at my table. I was eating alone, as usual.

"So, inquiring minds want to know. What makes me such an asshole?"

"That shirt." I put down the Tater Tot I was about to eat. "It's totally sick."

"It is not."

"It makes me want to puke."

"I thought it was more like a tribute." The guy sounded thoughtful. "I saw it in the music store at the mall last night, and I thought—I wanted something to wear today to let people know that we shouldn't forget about Kurt." He swallowed. "I really loved Nirvana."

"Me too." I felt like I was going to cry. The news just broke that weekend, and I'd stayed up all Sunday night watching the tributes on MTV. That Monday was the first day back from spring break, but instead of talking about their vacations, all anybody could talk about was Kurt. Even the kids who liked Pearl Jam better than Nirvana. Nobody was going to forget Kurt.

"What about this?" The guy was taking his shirt off. He was sitting right there in the cafeteria without a shirt on. He turned the shirt inside out and put it back on. The tag stuck out in the back. He held out his arms. "Better?"

"Yeah." I speared another Tater Tot with my fork and tried not to smile. "How come they haven't sent you home for uniform violation yet? Or made you put on another shirt?"

"I've already got two detentions," he said, grinning. "But they won't do anything else. They're afraid I'm too upset. I might do something *crazy.*" His eyes got wide.

I laughed. Maybe he wasn't so bad after all.

"I won't wear it anymore. You have my word."

"Okay."

"I'm Brian, by the way."

"Maria."

"I know. We had study hall together last semester."

"Oh. Oh yeah." I kind of remembered him now. "Mr. Kilgore."

He nodded and stole one of my Tater Tots. "So, what's your favorite Nirvana song?"

That was the start of Brian and I becoming best friends. I'd just started at Langley, and I hadn't exactly hit it off with most of the girls there. They were all into boys and makeup and going to the mall, and they had a lot more money to spend there than I did. All I wanted to do was hang out and listen to music, and that's pretty much all Brian and his friends did, too. We played tapes and rode skateboards and cracked jokes. It was always a lot of fun, up until this past summer. Maybe we were just getting older or something. Maybe boys and girls really couldn't be friends. All I know is that, around the end of tenth grade, hanging out with Brian stopped being fun and started being a big drag. A big drag that felt dangerous sometimes. Lately, hanging out with Brian and his friends, it felt like my throat was being squeezed so tightly I could barely breathe.

It was almost three in the afternoon on my first real day in New York City. Mom and Travis were asleep. I wasn't sure what time they'd gotten home, but they were still gone when I went to bed a little past midnight. Now I was itching to explore the city, but I didn't want to wake them up, and I wasn't so sure about going out by myself, without a key. Also, I was starving. I found a stale Entenmann's doughnut to eat for breakfast, but it was the only one left, and there wasn't much else in the kitchen besides spaghetti noodles and beer. I was almost to the point of eating the noodles dry just to keep my stomach from growling.

Finally the bedroom door opened, and Travis stumbled through the beaded curtain into the bathroom. I concentrated on the subway maps I was studying and tried not to listen to him pee. When he came out, he saw me awake. He didn't have a shirt on, and I could see the tattoo over his heart that read AILEEN. His hair was slicked down, and it made him look shorter. He yawned and stretched. I kept my eyes on the maps.

"Hey. What's up?" he asked.

"Not much. How was the show?"

"It was pretty rad. It's Lou, you know."

I nodded like I knew.

"You got it all figured out yet?" He glanced toward my maps.

"I dunno. Is Eighty-Second Street far from here?"

"Yeah, it's far. Why'd you want to go all the way up there?" He picked up a T-shirt hanging off the back of one of the kitchen chairs and sniffed it.

"That's where the school is. I have to be there at eight in the morning."

"We could ride up there and check it out." He pulled the T-shirt on. It was tight and black and said VIVE LE ROCK in white letters.

"What about Mom?"

"She's got her, uh, thing today. One of her meetings. You know, AA or whatever."

"I didn't know she drank."

"She doesn't anymore." Travis bent over to tug his boots on. "Hence the meetings." He put on a fraying denim jacket with a patch on the sleeve that was a profile of a skull. Ran his hand through his hair. "You wanna go get something to eat?"

"Yeah." I got up and pulled on my black hooded sweatshirt. My army surplus boots were already on.

"You expecting company?" Travis looked at me and snickered.

"What?"

"You could fit, like, three more people into those pants."

"They're JNCOs," I said. Everybody wore JNCOs back home. Superbaggy skater jeans. Maybe they weren't cool in New York, though.

"And you're about to lose your sole." He pointed at my right boot. I lifted my foot. I hadn't even noticed. The sole had finally detached from the rest of the boot and flopped down, exposing the dingy inner lining. Travis went to the kitchen and opened a drawer. He pulled out a roll of duct tape and tossed it at me. I caught it awkwardly and picked at the edges, trying to pull some off the roll.

"Here, gimme that." He came over and snatched it out of my hands. "And you're not even the one with the hangover." He smiled and pulled a long strip off the roll, tearing it with his teeth. "Lift up." He patted my right leg, and I steadied myself on his shoulders as he bent down to tape up my shoe.

"All right, now you're ready for action." He patted my leg again and stood up. I looked down at the new silver strip capping the toe of my boot. He tossed the tape onto the kitchen counter. "One more thing, then we're ready." He crept back into the bed-room and came out holding two motorcycle helmets. He handed me one of them.

"What's this for?"

"This is a dangerous city," he said. Then he cracked up. "You should see the look on your face." He opened the door. "Come on, it's for my bike."

"Your bike?"

"Motorcycle. Whatever. You're cool on a motorcycle, right?"

"I, uh . . ." I'd never been on a motorcycle in my life. But I didn't want to be uncool, on a motorcycle or not. "I guess we'll see."

It was Sunday afternoon and everything was open, doors propped and signs calling out: GYRO LOTTERY PSYCHIC ADVISER NAILS KEYS 99 CENTS INDIAN FOOD. I followed Travis through the streets of the Lower East Side to another diner, where we stuffed ourselves silly on French toast and bacon. We ate quickly and silently, then went back out onto the street, past the cleaners and tailors and the newspapers in thick stacks outside bodega windows, signs in Spanish taped beneath the ones in English. We passed kids in tight black pants who looked like rock stars, young men in sharp black jackets and sunglasses, old women dressed like Halloween gypsies shuffling behind carts full of laundry bundles with small dogs balanced on top. It was almost four in the afternoon, and the sun was sinking in the sky.

"I love when it starts getting dark early," he said. "I wish it was nighttime all the time, you know?"

"I know what you mean." I swung the motorcycle helmet as we walked. "It's like everything's more secretive or something."

"So where did you guys use to live? You grew up here, right?"

"I can't remember," I told him. "We moved when I was two."

"That sucks." We stopped by a skinny tree with a looped chain around it. Travis's motorcycle was parked next to it. A small black Honda, the letters in gold. He knelt down to undo the lock. "I grew up across the river. Over in Queens. Same place as Johnny Thunders. I don't guess they taught you about Johnny Thunders down there in South Carolina, did they?" He stood up, coiling the chain around his forearm.

"Sure they did. He invented the cotton gin, right?"

Travis looked at me and laughed.

"No? Not the cotton gin? Louisiana Purchase, then. Women's suffrage? The Teapot Dome Scandal?"

"Come on." He straddled the bike, still laughing. "Wait, where are we going, again?"

"Eighty-Second Street, between Lexington and Park Avenue." I put on the helmet and swung my leg over the bike. There was nothing to hang on to but Travis. I circled my arms around his ribs. He cranked the engine and it popped and huffed.

"You better hold on tighter than that," he warned me. "Unless you wanna leave half your brains back on Avenue C." He cackled and cut the wheel. We sped out into the street, and I clung to him, instinctively, for dear life.

"So I guess this is it." I hopped off the bike and took off the helmet. Prince Academy. It didn't look too bad. It was just a regular brick building, sitting there in the same block as all the other dark brick buildings. The only things that set it apart were the set of marble steps out front and the white flag waving with the Prince Academy logo in royal blue and gold.

"Prince Academy? That's the name of the place?" Travis turned the bike off. A taxi honked as it sped by, and he pulled up closer to the curb. "Forget Johnny Thunders. They're gonna teach you all about *Purple Rain*."

"Yeah. And wait till you see the uniform. It's all ruffles and lace."

Travis laughed. He got off the bike. "You start tomorrow morning?"

I nodded.

"Maybe, uh." Travis scratched his head. "I know Vic's not much of a morning person. But maybe we could come up here with you. Or whatever. You know, on your first day."

"That's okay," I told him. "I'm used to doing it on my own." My dad wasn't really a hands-on guy back at home. I had long since learned to forge his signature on permission slips and report cards. I took my bike or, if it was raining, called Brian for a ride. I hadn't gone to school with a parent holding my hand since third grade.

"Afraid it'll ruin your reputation?" Travis sniffed. "Rich kids see you pull up on the back of some guy's motorcycle, think you're one of the bad girls?"

"I'm not worried about the rich kids," I said, walking up the marble steps and tugging on the locked wooden door. I guess I should have been more nervous, but I wasn't. I guess after Langley, after everything that had happened with Brian, nothing bothered me anymore. Maybe it had all toughened me up somehow. I hoped that it had.

"Are you embarrassed about it?" Travis asked. I turned and walked back down the steps. "Me and your mom?"

"What do you mean?"

"I mean, I'm only six years older than you are." He leaned against the bike. "Do you think it's weird that I'm dating her?"

"Look, I'm not gonna call you 'Dad' or anything. But as long as you care about her, I don't care how old you are." I looked at him. "I'm just used to doing things on my own. You guys don't have to pack my lunch and help me find my homeroom, or whatever. It's eleventh grade. I think I can deal."

"You can deal, huh?" He shook his head. "I gotta hand it to you, Maria. You got your shit together a lot more than I did when I was your age. Either that, or you've got a heck of a bluff. First time I came to the city I didn't know up from down, and it scared the hell out of me. And I'm from Queens, not Ass Scratch, Carolina, or wherever it is."

"My grandmother lives in Atlanta. We're down there every month. It's not like I've never seen a skyscraper."

"All right, hot shot. Which train you taking tomorrow morning?"

"The, uh—" I thought back to the subway map I'd been studying all morning. I still couldn't remember all the numbers and letters. "The green one."

"The green one." He shook his head again and got back on the bike. "Let's get out of here."

"Where are we going now?"

"We're getting out of this neighborhood before somebody pulls up in a Rolls-Royce and asks me for some Grey Poupon." He cranked the engine. "And I'm gonna teach you up from down." He looked over his shoulder, and we were off again.

We drove back downtown, weaving around cabs and cars and delivery trucks and people rushing out into the crosswalks.

Travis drove us all the way down to Battery Park first, to see the water and the Statue of Liberty all lit up as the sun went down. We rode back up past the World Trade Center. He told me if I ever got lost downtown, the Twin Towers are south and the Empire State Building is north. South is down, north is up.

"Above the Empire State Building, you're on your own," he said.

We wove through the crooked streets of the West Village, down Canal Street, through Chinatown and the cobblestone streets of SoHo. Then we went up to Union Square, and Travis showed me where Andy Warhol's Factory used to be. We circled around back to Bleecker Street until we dead-ended at CBGBs, a little bar with a dingy brown awning.

"You gotta ask your mom to tell you her CBs stories," Travis said. "She used to see everybody down here when she was a kid. Ramones, Johnny Thunders, Patti Smith. Everybody."

I wished my mom was there. I wondered what she was doing. How long she'd been going to AA meetings. I didn't know she had a drinking problem. That was probably why my dad and my grandmother were so uptight about me moving up here. Maybe I should tell them she was going to meetings now. Maybe they'd know that she was different. That she'd changed.

"Come on." Travis parked the bike. "Let's go to the Punk Rock Mall."

"The Punk Rock Mall?"

I followed Travis up to St. Marks Place, where there were rows of shops full of punk rock gear, black T-shirts with band names on them like Crass and D.O.A., plaid pants with tons of zippers, Doc Martens. There were people selling books and bootleg videos on the street, girls with nose rings handing out flyers for discount tattoos and piercings, punks and bums and kids younger than me all running in and out of the shops, different music blasting out of each open door. I felt like I couldn't stop looking at everything, and everything begged to be looked at. Everyone wanted to be seen.

"Let's go spin the cube." Travis snagged my sleeve and we ran across the street, just making the light. There was a concrete island in the middle of the crisscrossing streets with a sculpture of a big cube sitting in the middle of it. All around us, skaters did kickflips off the curb.

"Take a corner!" Travis pushed against the edge of the big black cube, which seemed to balance on one of its pointed corners. Some kids with dreadlocks and leather jackets were sitting beneath the cube. They looked at us warily, then got up and walked away.

"Are you serious?"

"Yeah! Start pushing!" Travis leaned into the cube, putting all his weight into it.

"Like this?" I pushed against another one of the edges. There was a little give. Sure enough, the cube started to move. Pretty soon it loosened up, and we walked in a slow circle, pushing the cube, trying to work up to a run. The dreadlocked kids came back and helped, and then we really got it going. Finally we all collapsed, laughing. The cube grunted to a halt. Travis wiped his hands on his pant legs and spit.

"You hungry?" he asked.

"Sorta," I said. It had been awhile since the French toast and bacon.

"Let's go get the bike and we'll ride over to MacDougal Street."

"What's on MacDougal Street?" I fell into step with him at the crosswalk.

"The best falafels in town."

"What's a falafel?"

Travis laughed. I didn't care. I just jammed my hands into my sweatshirt pocket and followed him, wherever he would lead.

There was a note from Mom when we got home with our sack of falafels. This one was sketched with little cars in the corners, the words made to look like they were forming out of the puffy clouds of exhaust.

Hi guys!
I'll be out late tonite—sorry! But guess what?
Repo Man's on TV! Go get sushi and don't pay!
Love, Vic

"Why does she want us to steal sushi?" I asked.

"You never saw *Repo Man*?"

"No."

"It's a line in the movie. Anyway, we got falafels." Travis took one of the foil-wrapped falafels out of the bag and handed it to me. I was disappointed. I was looking forward to hanging out with my mom. I looked at my watch. Dad wanted me to call him when I got to the train station and again when I got to Mom's. I'd been so glad that Mom and Travis even showed up—

and that I didn't have to call Dad and tell him he was right—that I forgot to call and tell him everything was okay.

Halfway through the movie, I dialed his number. I waited until I knew he had gone to work. I don't know why, but I didn't feel like talking to him. So I left a message.

"Hi, Dad . . . it's me. I just wanted to let you know I got in okay. Sorry I didn't call you last night, but there's been a lot to do, getting ready for school and all." I twisted the cord around my finger, looking through the kitchen at Travis. He was drinking beer and laughing at the movie. "And, uh, Mom's been showing me around. So I guess I'll call you tomorrow night and let you know how it's going."

I couldn't think of anything else. But then, at the last minute, I remembered to tell him that I loved him.

3

I took a moment on the marble steps of Prince Academy to tug my skirt down again and wonder if I'd just made a terribly rash decision. A wave of fear ran through me like a shock, and I almost wished I'd stayed at Langley, even if it meant dodging Brian and those guys for an entire year. I wished I'd at least taken Travis up on his offer to give me a ride. But I knew, at some point, I had to go in there and get it over with on my own. I took a deep breath. What was I so afraid of, anyway? Everything had worked out. I told my father and my grandmother that I wanted out, and they finally listened. Prince Academy was my salvation. They made a special exception, since the year had already started. They made an exception because I had good grades and my grandmother had lots of money. It was a combination that could get you all kinds of places, evidently.

Well, grades, money, and a class-A freak-out.

I pulled on the heavy wooden door, and this time it swung

open. My skirt was too short. I was too tall. At least the uniforms were a little nicer than the ones at Langley, but the rules were more strict. Dress shoes or loafers, no exceptions. Langley famously had no uniform policy on shoes, so that was where everybody let their personalities hang out.

The halls were quiet. I knew I was late. My new loafers pinched my toes. I found the school office. All the receptionists stopped and looked at me when I walked in. You really can't sneak up on anybody when you're five foot ten.

"Hi, um. I'm new. Today's my first day. Maria Costello."

"Have a seat." One of the receptionists pointed to a row of plastic chairs, and I sat. As soon as I did, someone called my name.

"Maria Costello?" I looked up. There was a woman in a pin-striped suit standing over me with a handful of papers.

"Yeah? Yes, ma'am?" I stood up. I was taller than she was.

"I'm not old enough to be a ma'am yet, am I?" She looked up at me and frowned.

"I was—I just meant—" I backpedaled.

"Don't worry about it. I'm Mrs. Alvarez. I'm the assistant principal." She walked out of the office, her heels clipping along. I followed, double time. "Come along. I'll show you to your locker and homeroom. You're late."

"I know." I slung my backpack full of empty binders and notebooks over my shoulder. "I'm still learning the subway." I'd gotten on in the wrong direction and almost ended up in Brooklyn.

"It's fine for today. You'll learn to budget your time pretty quickly here. The city will force you. This is your locker." She barely paused. "The combination's here, along with your

schedule. You came to us from . . . South Dakota, am I right?"
She handed me the sheaf of papers in her hand.

"South Carolina." I tried to read the papers as we walked.

"Not close at all, was I? There's also a map of the school,
though I believe you received one of those in the package we
sent."

"Yes, ma— Yes."

"The first-period bell is going to ring in another minute or
two. Mr. Dunleavy is your homeroom teacher, and this"—she
stopped in front of a closed wooden door—"is his classroom."
She opened the door and scuttled me in.

"Mr. Dunleavy, your new student."

Mrs. Alvarez left, closing the door behind her. The papers
she'd given me were crumpling in my sweaty hand. Mr. Dunleavy sat on the edge of his desk, calling the roll. The classroom
was big, and the kids were all looking at me.

"Class, our new import, Maria Costello." He gave me a smile.
He was a young guy with wire-rimmed glasses and a beard.
"Maria, since you're already standing, why don't you tell us
where you're from and what you like to do."

"Well, um, I'm from South Carolina. But I was born here.
And, uh. I just like to hang out. Listen to music. You know,
whatever."

"Okay, guys, I'm sure you'll all be your usual wonderful
selves and help Maria get acclimated to her new surroundings
here at Prince. Now—oh, Maria, you can have a seat."

I moved down the aisle, feeling huge, and sat at the first
empty desk I saw as Mr. Dunleavy finished calling the roll. The
bell rang before he got through the list.

"Okay, guys, if you're not here, please see me before first period," he announced, and the kids laughed. While everybody else filed out I stayed in my seat, checking the schedule against the map of the school, trying to figure out where I was supposed to go next.

At lunch, I saw a girl I recognized from my first-period English class who seemed pretty cool. She had dyed-black hair and black fingernail polish and she held court at a table with an empty seat, so I sat down.

"Is it okay if I—"

"It's cool," she said, moving her tray aside. "Mary, right?"

"Maria."

"I'm Tracy. This is Danae, Cassidy, and Rebekah."

"Hey." Already I was wondering if I said something wrong. None of these girls was smiling. They looked older than me, and their makeup and hair were all perfect. Even Tracy's black fingernail polish didn't have a single chip. Maybe I should've just kept walking.

"You're in my homeroom," Danae said, as if she were accusing me of something. "So, what kind of music are you into?"

"Oh, um—pretty much everything—"

"Reggae? Smooth jazz? French hip-hop?" Danae shot back. Rebekah, tall and freckled, snorted a laugh.

"Mainly just, you know, rock music." I swallowed. Suddenly I didn't feel like eating. "Nirvana. Jeff Buckley. Liz Phair. Sonic Youth—"

"We just saw Sonic Youth." Tracy came to my rescue.

"Oh my gosh, they were so *boring*." Cassidy giggled. "It

39

was, like, two hours of guitars going *rrrrrwwwwwaaaarrrrr*. And then we had to go back and be nice to them."

"My dad works at Sony," Tracy explained. "He gets us backstage passes."

"Please." Danae shook her head, chewing a mouthful of cafeteria cheeseburger. "Explain Sonic Youth to us. Because we were so, like, *whatever*."

"They're, um . . ." I stabbed a dried-out french fry with my fork. *Dory, where are you when I need you?* "They're, like, kind of experimental. Sometimes their songs are just, like, noise. But they have regular songs, too. Like on *Dirty*. And *Goo*. And, um, *Daydream Nation* is good, too. It's, uh . . . I think they just have a lot of feedback because it's like . . . maybe they're trying to make it up as they go along?" *Yeah. I suck at this.*

"Guys, you have to admit, it was better than when my dad got us tickets to Mariah Carey," Tracy said.

"No! I love Mariah Carey!" Rebekah protested.

"You would." Danae rolled her eyes.

"Whatever." Rebekah shoved Danae. "You're the one who listens to the Spice Girls."

"No comment," Danae said, closing her eyes. "It's well-crafted modern pop."

"Next time I get Sonic Youth tickets, I'll give them to you," Tracy told me.

"Is your dad getting us into the R.E.M. show next month?" Cassidy asked.

"It's a done deal," Tracy said.

Cassidy squealed. "I love Michael Stipe!" She clapped her hands. "Ooh, I can't wait to meet him. He's so cute!"

"Ew, no." Rebekah crinkled her nose. "He's bald."

"Bald guys are hot," Cassidy said. "I'm into Moby, too."

"Cass, you are officially weird," Rebekah said.

"Okay." Tracy stood up, crumpling her lunch bag. "Ten minutes till sixth period. Who's ready to go out for a smoke?"

I hurried to finish my french fries as the rest of the girls gathered their purses and trays and stood up.

"See you around, Mary." Tracy smiled at me, and I realized I wasn't invited.

Dear Dory, I wrote as the subway slung my handwriting all over the page. *Why do we need Algebra I, let alone Algebra II? Didn't the* Rocky *movies teach us that sequels are bad? Also, today's lunchtime pop quiz: Explain why Sonic Youth is not boring. My rich, gorgeous classmates hung out with Kim, Thurston, Lee, and Steve, and all I got was this lousy T-shirt.*

The subway ride down from the Upper East Side to the Spring Street stop was pretty long, but it gave me time to catch up on my homework. It was probably a good thing my budding social life looked pretty bleak. I couldn't slack off if I wanted to stay at Prince. Already I was under the gun; I had a week to read *Their Eyes Were Watching God* before the midterm, when all the other kids had had an entire month. *And* figure out quadratic equations. But I could sit there on the subway with the other New Yorkers with their papers and their paperbacks, sipping their coffees, pretending like I didn't even notice that we're on a train underground going what felt like eighty miles an hour. And that was pretty cool.

As cool as the subway ride was, I liked walking in the city even more. I liked the big brick buildings in SoHo; I liked the people with their sidewalk stands selling jewelry and hot dogs and cheap bootleg CDs. I liked watching the people—the kids with Mohawks carrying guitar cases, the guys in Jets jerseys unloading trucks, the women walking dogs dressed in little outfits. I probably saw more people in one afternoon as I walked home than I ever saw in my entire life in Millville.

I got to the apartment and made the final climb up the stairs. I could smell spicy food cooking, hear Oprah coming from behind the doors, voices speaking in Spanish and laughing. But the fifth floor was strangely quiet. As I got closer to our door, I could hear women's voices. Women shouting. I pulled the long chain out of my shirt collar, the one with the apartment keys and the emergency subway token on it. When I unlocked the door and opened it, the voices got louder. I stood in the doorway, hesitating.

"I mean, Jesus, Nina, two weeks!" The voice was edgy, almost hysterical. My mother's voice. "What am I supposed to do? I don't know how you expect me to—"

"Victoria, you're not the only person in the world who—" The other voice, the calmer, quieter voice, got even quieter. I couldn't hear what she was saying. I closed the door behind me. Travis was sitting on the futon, plucking an electric guitar that wasn't plugged in to anything. The strings made faint plinking noises, almost like a toy.

"Hey," I whispered, tiptoeing over. "What's going on?"

"The landlord," Travis whispered back. He looked up at me. "You play?"

"Guitar? No." I always wanted to. A few years ago, my grandmother was cleaning out her house, and she found an old acoustic guitar in the attic, gathering dust. She put it in a big pile of stuff she wanted my dad to haul off to the Salvation Army, but I persuaded him to let me take the guitar home. I asked him to book me a lesson at the music school across town, but when the day came, he forgot about it and went to work. It was too far for me to walk, and I couldn't bike with the guitar. Dad apologized and booked me another lesson, but he forgot that one, too. After that, I didn't ask for any more lessons. And now the guitar sat in the hall closet of our house in Millville, gathering more dust.

"Here. Sit down." Travis patted the futon next to him. I sat, and he slid the guitar into my lap. It was heavier than I thought it would be.

"Hold it like this." He propped it up and put the pick in my right hand. "Now press down on the strings with your left hand, like this." He made my hand into a claw and pressed my fingertips down on the strings.

"Ow!"

"Now strum with the pick." I strummed. The notes buzzed out, nowhere near how I thought they would sound. Travis moved one of my fingers. I pressed harder and strummed again. This time, it sounded better.

"There you go. That's pretty good," he whispered.

I had to let go. "It hurts!"

"You've gotta build up your calluses. I've got pretty heavy strings on here, too." He took the guitar back and played a quick succession of notes. I couldn't believe how fast his fingers moved on the strings.

Just then the bedroom door burst open, and we both looked up. A tall woman with sleek black hair and a scarf swept over her shoulders walked out into the kitchen. My mom was behind her. She looked like she'd been crying.

"And you must be Maria." The woman looked at me. "I'm Nina Dowd, an old friend of your mother's."

"Pleased to meet you." I stood up and shook her hand, out of politeness. Her name sounded familiar. I was trying to remember when my mother had mentioned her before, but I couldn't. I didn't know why, but I felt like this woman was the enemy.

"You just started at Prince Academy, right?"

"Yes, ma'am." Behind Nina, in the kitchen, my mother lit a cigarette. *Nina.* She was the one who owned the boutique where my mother worked—that's what it was. It was in one of her letters, maybe two years ago. *I'm working in my friend Nina's boutique. Part-time, so I can still do my art.*

"My late husband's alma mater. How do you like it?"

"Today was my first day." Wait a minute. Suddenly, I remembered. Nina Dowd. She was my grandmother's friend, the one whose telephone number my grandmother gave me when I left. The one I was supposed to call if I needed anything. Okay, so how was it remotely possible that my mother and my grandmother had the same friend? Maybe there were two different women named Nina Dowd. That made way more sense.

"Ah, well, it seems you've emerged in one piece."

"I guess so."

"Victoria." Nina ended our conversation abruptly. "I have an appointment. You know where to reach me." She turned back to face me. "Maria, it was lovely to meet you."

"Likewise," I said. She walked out the door in a cloud of citrusy perfume. As soon as she left, my mother started crying. Travis leaped off the couch and went to put his arms around her.

"What happened, babe? What is it?"

She buried her face in his chest, shaking her head. I felt like I should leave. Like something was happening between the two of them that I shouldn't be watching.

"I thought I was getting better." She was choking on tears. "Wasn't I doing better?"

"You're doing great, honey," Travis murmured. "What did she tell you?"

Mom sniffled and straightened up. She smiled a strange smile.

"Nina," she said, her voice dripping, poisonous, "is selling the building. The new owners are raising the rent." She shook her head. "I can't believe it. I've been living here since 1987, and she's never raised the rent once. Not once. And now she's going to let somebody waltz right in here and take the shirts off our backs."

"How much are you paying now?" I asked.

"Two hundred and fifty a month."

"Does she know how much these new people are gonna raise it?" Travis asked.

"Maybe it's not that much," I said. Mom shook her head, wiping mascara off her cheeks. I was already calculating in my head. I was happy to help out with the rent. I could ask my grandmother for some money to make up the difference, and then, once I got caught up at Prince, I could get a part-time job.

"Fifteen fifty a month."

"Fifteen *hundred* and fifty dollars?" Travis exploded. "For this place? That's bullshit!"

"Are you sure?" I asked. "That seems like way too much."

"It's the way the whole city is going." Mom looked at me

warily. "You get a mayor like Giuliani, who decides to get tough on crime and turns Times Square into some kind of amusement park, and all the people who moved out to the suburbs because they thought the city wasn't safe decide to move back because now they turn on *Regis and Kathie Lee* or whatever and, oh, it looks like so much *fun*. 'Look honey, no more hookers! Let's go see a show and take the kids!' But it's fake! It's cheap and plastic and fake, and now it's happening down here—used to be, you couldn't walk through this neighborhood in broad daylight without having to look over your shoulder. But, I'm telling you, Rivington Street's gonna end up just another theme-park ride, like Times Square. Someplace only trust-fund babies can afford. Someplace they can come play Make-Believe Artist until they decide to take over their parents' companies. But it's totally phony. It's Bohemians of the Caribbean!"

Travis laughed. Mom kept ranting.

"You think it's funny?" Mom ripped a paper towel off the roll and blew her nose. "Think about all the people we know who stuck it out down here all these years, and now they're losing their stores and apartments from the rent going up."

"What happens to them?" I felt nervous again, imagining us like the people I'd seen on the streets. Homeless. At least I had Millville to go back to, even though I didn't want to. But Mom and Travis couldn't exactly come move in with my dad.

"What happens is that they have to leave the city," Mom explained. "Move out to the boroughs. Or New Jersey. And I'll be damned if I'm moving back there." My mom was born and raised in New Jersey. But, according to my dad, she and her father, my grandfather, didn't get along. Her mom died when she was little, and her father remarried a woman who ended up being the classic evil stepmother. It was strange to think that I had a grandfather I'd never even met.

"We could go stay at my dad's place for a while," Travis offered. "Out in Forest Hills. At least until I can get a job again."

"What about the boutique?" I asked.

"Huh?"

"Yeah, what about the *boutique*." Travis gave Mom a funny look.

"I mean . . . this is the same Nina who's your boss, right?"

"Right. How did you know that?"

"You wrote about her. In a letter you sent me," I reminded her. "Anyway, she can't expect you to come to work when you don't have any place to live."

"Oh, believe me, Nina's taken care of everything. Out of the goodness of her heart." Mom's voice got sarcastic again. "She's offered us an apartment in Brooklyn. At the bargain-basement price of four hundred and fifty dollars a month."

"We can pull off four-fifty," Travis decided. "And Brooklyn's not so bad. The guys from the band used to live out there, before they moved to LA."

"*Parts* of Brooklyn aren't so bad." Mom rolled her eyes. "It's the apartment above Citygirls."

"You gotta be kidding me." Travis laughed.

"What's Citygirls?" I asked.

"It's a—" Mom grimaced. "Strip club. It belonged to Nina's late husband."

"It's right under the BQE!" Travis exclaimed. "Between that and the music, how are we ever gonna get any sleep at night?"

"Oh, you sleep through everything," Mom scoffed. "Jack-hammers, thunderstorms—"

"What's the BQE?" I interrupted.

"Brooklyn-Queens Expressway," Mom explained. "You'll get to know it intimately. We have to be out of here in two weeks."

"I refuse to be depressed about this," Mom announced after we'd all moped around the apartment. I joined in the moping wholeheartedly once I looked up the nearest stop to the new apartment on the subway map and realized that my ride to school had just doubled in length.

"We're ordering out for dinner." She yanked open a kitchen drawer and got out a stack of menus. "You two order anything you want. Order everything. I don't care." She handed the menus to Travis and grabbed her purse. "I'll be right back. I'm going to get us some drinks." Mom whirled out the door. As soon as it was closed, she flung it open again.

"And put some music on, for Pete's sake," she added, then left again.

"All right." Travis smiled. "Here, find us some food." He handed the menus off to me and leaped over the edge of the futon toward the stereo. A blast of guitar came out of the speakers. The Ramones. Travis cranked it even louder and started to pogo dance. He pogoed back into the kitchen, right into me.

"Knock it off, I'm making dinner." I elbowed him. There were too many choices. New Dragon Chinese, Burritos-to-Go, Mikoto Sushi, JJ's Pizzeria, the Hummus House.

"Let's get something from everywhere," Travis said, already breathless. He pogoed into me again, and I shoved back.

"Okay, Mosh Pit, just because we're getting kicked out doesn't mean we should destroy the place."

"Yes it does!" Travis was jubilant.

"Will you stop bouncing and help me order dinner? What do you want, anyway?"

"Pancakes." He laughed. "Pancakes and pizza and a Burrito to Go!"

"Oh my gosh, it's, like, twenty till two!" Mom giggled, shoving the empty food containers into a trash bag. "What time do you have to be up for school?"

"Six thirty," I said. We both burst out laughing. Travis ended up drinking the beer she bought, even though she offered me one—since I wasn't driving, she said. I decided to stick to the spicy Jamaican ginger beer my mom bought for herself. Nonalcoholic, for that pure-cane-sugar buzz.

"I guess I should let you get to sleep," she said. "It's only your second day."

"I'm not tired, though."

"Me neither!" She tossed the trash bag into the corner. "Let's learn how to Pony!" She put another tape in the VCR. Mom had a whole stack of these tapes of old dance shows from the sixties, like *Shindig!* and *Hullabaloo*. We'd already learned the Mashed Potato, the Watusi, the Hully Gully, the Hitch Hike, and the Swim. Now she pressed play and we tried to follow the smiling girls in Patty Duke hairdos showing us the steps. Pretty soon we were falling into each other and laughing again.

"Shh, we're gonna wake up Travis," I cautioned.

"Don't worry about him. Seriously, he really has slept through jackhammers." She turned the TV down anyway. "So, I haven't had a chance to ask you what you think."

"I think we're going to have to practice a lot more if we're going to take this show on the road." I pointed at the girls doing the Pony flawlessly on the screen.

"No, silly." She laughed, bumping my shoulder. "What do you think about Travis?"

"I like him. He's nice."

"I know. And he's so hot. Wait till you see him play guitar."

I concentrated on the TV so Mom wouldn't see me blushing. It was embarrassing to hear her talk about Travis being hot.

"But do you think he's too young?" she asked. "He's only twenty-two. I'm, like, two years younger than his *mom*. Is that too weird?"

"I dunno." Truthfully, it didn't seem too weird at all. Maybe because my mom seemed so young herself. "He's younger than Dad, that's for sure."

"Honey, everybody's younger than your dad," she said. "How is the old man, anyway?"

"The same." I didn't know why I brought him up. I shoved aside the stacks of records we'd pulled out earlier and sat down on the edge of the futon, finally out of breath from the dancing.

"You okay?" She sat down next to me.

"Yeah, I'm just tired." I rolled my ankles around and yawned. I guess I could've said more on my dad's behalf. But there was nothing I could tell my mom about him that was going to make her change her mind all of a sudden and run down to Millville to get back together with him. So what was the point?

"He's not seeing anybody?" she asked. "Your dad, I mean."

"Not really. He dated this waitress a while back. Last year. They went out for a month or two. Just to the movies and stuff. Then she broke up with him or something. I dunno. He doesn't really talk to me about it."

"What about your love life?"

"What about it?"

"You tell me! Any secret crushes at school? Boyfriends back home you're pining away for?" She raised her eyebrows at me.

"I've only been at Prince one day. And there's no— There's not anybody back home."

"Well, give it time. Who knows? Over at that school, you'll probably end up meeting some Saudi Arabian prince, and next thing you know you'll be heiress to an oil fortune!"

"And then I'll buy the building back!" I laughed, but Mom's eyes dropped, and she looked sad again.

"Kiddo." She ruffled my hair. "I'm glad you're around."

"Thanks." I looked down at my hands. "I mean, seriously. Thanks for letting me come stay with you."

"Oh my gosh, we're gonna have so much fun." She yawned and stood up. "Let's do one more, okay?" She pulled me to my feet. "The Alligator, and then we hit the sack."

We got used to staying up all night last summer. Brian and I, plus Donald and his girlfriend, Bonnie, and our friend Ben, and whoever else he could wrangle. We'd go hang out at the abandoned bowling alley sometimes, but mostly we'd go to the woods near Ben's house. The guys built a little half-pipe skate ramp out there, and we'd spend all night beneath the tall pines, skating and drinking beer that Donald bought with his fake ID. We'd get a bonfire going, turn the radio on, and stay up till dawn, when we'd go to Waffle House, or have chicken biscuits with the early-morning old-timers down at Hardee's.

By July, I was tired. It seemed like everything was getting split up, like I was two different people depending on who I was with. Dory was home from college in Athens, so when I'd go down to my grandmother's house, she would get me into Club Mod, this crazy gay club where we'd dance all night and hang out with the drag queens. They were catty and funny and smart, not like Brian and the guys. I didn't tell Dory about Brian, and I didn't tell Brian too much about Dory. Dory would've thought Brian and the guys were stupid rednecks, and Brian already thought Dory was, in his words, "a dyke." He called her that when he saw all the mixtapes she made for me. I told him he didn't get it, but if I told him about going to gay clubs with her, well, he *really* wouldn't get that.

Plus, Brian and I had kind of started dating. It was my own fault, I guess. We got bored one night and started fooling around. I didn't want to sleep with him, though. He started calling me more often after that, and the two of us started spending more time together on our own. By the time August rolled around, he was getting more and more insistent, wanting to know why I wouldn't sleep with him. I told him it was because I was Catholic, and that shut him up for a while. The more we were together, the more I realized that just because we both liked Nirvana and skateboarding didn't mean I wanted him for a boyfriend. I wasn't even sure I wanted him for just a friend.

"He sounds like a drag," Dory said when I finally told her about him. It was the last weekend before we both went back to school. I thought I wouldn't see Dory again until Thanksgiving. Neither of us knew then that I'd end up back in Atlanta in just a few weeks' time.

"I'm kind of bored with it," I admitted. We were hanging

out in Dory's room. I was reading back issues of *Sassy* magazine while Dory made a mixtape for someone back in Athens. "But he likes me. And we're friends, besides."

"Big deal." She flipped the tape over. "I'm friends with a lot of people, but I'm not gonna hop into bed with them. You don't *have* to sleep with anybody. Especially at your age."

"There are ninth graders at my school who sleep around."

"So what? They're probably insecure and they think that's the only way anyone will like them. You're smarter and more interesting than that. Wait until you meet someone you really love. Someone who makes you feel special. Otherwise, it's not worth the drama."

I decided to take Dory's advice. I wasn't really in love with Brian. I planned to break up with him before school started. I planned to break up with the whole group, actually. After all three guys found out they'd made the varsity wrestling team back in the spring, it was like a spell came over them. Well, Ben was the same doofus as ever, but Brian and Donald got cocky over the summer. And once school started, it got even worse. They started walking around like they owned the place. They picked on underclassmen and started fights after school. I kept procrastinating, thinking that Brian would surely break up with me himself. But he never did. Finally, during the second week of school, the first wrestling match of the year came. They won decisively. I figured this was the time to break up with him. He was in such a good mood, he probably wouldn't even notice.

We were sitting in his truck, out in the woods. There was a bonfire going outside, and tons of kids, more than just our usual group.

"Brian, I was thinking about you and me," I started.

"Yeah, I was, too," he said.

Maybe this would be easier than I thought. "Well." I pulled at the door handle, nervous. "I was just thinking maybe we should take a little time off."

"Time off what?" He took a swig of his beer.

"I mean, like, maybe we should go back to being friends for a while. Go back to just hanging out."

"What the hell," he swirled the beer around in the can. "Seeing as how you won't sleep with me, we're pretty much just hanging out now, aren't we?" There was a hard edge to his voice. For the first time, I felt scared to be alone with him.

"Brian, come on—"

"I don't get you, Maria. I mean, you come on to me, but you don't wanna sleep with me, and now you decide you wanna break up altogether. And I ain't never done anything to you. I'd sleep with you, if you wanted to. How many other guys at this school you think you're gonna get?"

"I don't—I don't know." And I didn't care. I didn't want to sleep with anybody at Langley.

"You know what people are gonna say about you when they find out what a frigid little tease you are? When they find out about that dyke friend of yours down in Atlanta?"

"Brian, gimme a break." I rolled my eyes and opened the truck door. This was stupid. "This isn't working out. I'm done."

"You're not breaking up with me." He leaned over and grabbed the door handle, slamming the door shut. "You hear me? No fucking way are you breaking up with me. I'll tell everybody about you. You won't be able to walk through the goddam door at Langley."

"Brian—" I tried to laugh, but he fixed his glare on me, and I realized he wasn't kidding. A nauseous chill came over me. I looked past him, out the pickup window at the kids around the bonfire, the beer keg, the kids smoking joints in cupped hands. All I could think was, *How do I get out of this? How on earth did I get here, and how in the hell do I get out?*

4

"How was your day, dear?" Travis drawled in a nasal voice.

"Ehh, get me a beer," I growled. This was our little joke, the housewife and the businessman. Travis was always home when I got there, in between looking for jobs during the day and going to rehearsals at night. Mom picked up more hours at work, so we barely saw her in the weeks leading up to the move.

I took off my headphones and plunked my algebra book down on the kitchen table, next to a huge stack of records. Travis handed me a Dr. Brown's black cherry soda from the fridge. My new favorite drink, since you couldn't get Cheerwine in New York City. I poured it in a glass and went into the bathroom to take off my uniform.

"What's the deal with all those records?"

"They're Vic's. She's getting rid of them," Travis called out as I changed into my sweatshirt and jeans. I came back into the kitchen and hung my Prince blazer on the back of a chair.

Travis had put on my headphones and was listening to my Walkman.

"Who is this?" he said, loud over the music. I pulled one of the headphones away from his ear and leaned in to listen.

"Sleater-Kinney," I told him. "My friend Dory likes them a lot."

"Huh." Travis nodded his head in time to the music, then took the headphones off. "Chicks."

"*Huh, chicks*? What's that supposed to mean?"

"They're no Heartbreakers," he said, clicking the Walkman off. "I'm just sayin'."

"Huh. Dudes," I said in a *Beavis and Butt-head* voice. Travis elbowed me.

"You got homework?" he asked.

"Don't I always?"

"You gonna do it?"

"Don't I always?" I repeated. Prince Academy was turning out to be just as bad as Langley, maybe worse. The kids were even more stuck-up, completely ignoring me if I tried to start a conversation or sit with them in the cafeteria. The only strategy I could think of was just to buckle down, get good grades, and get out as fast as I could. That, and keep reminding myself that at least I was in New York City.

"Brainiac. You got time to help me with these records? I'm gonna give myself a hernia trying to carry them all."

"Sure. We're taking them down to the trash?"

"Nah, there's a place down the street that does buybacks on vinyl. You oughta go through 'em first, though. Vic said we could keep whatever we wanted."

"Why's she getting rid of all these?"

"Less to move. Extra money. The better to buy more records with." Travis grinned. I flipped through the stack. "She said it's all stuff people gave her that she doesn't like or stuff she's got two of."

I stopped flipping. In the upper left corner of a Kris Kristofferson album, I read my father's own cramped signature. *A. Costello*. Kris Kristofferson was his favorite. I looked through the rest, barely noticing the titles, just looking for his signature again. But there was only that one.

"You're keeping Kris Kristofferson?" Travis looked over my shoulder. I shrugged, defensive.

"There's some country music I like."

"You do, huh?" He grabbed an armful of records. "You know what you get when you play a country song backwards?"

"What?"

"You get your truck fixed, your dog comes back to life, and your mama gets out of prison."

"Ha, ha," I deadpanned, collecting the rest of the records.

"Shake a leg, willya?" He held the door open with his foot. "These things don't get any lighter."

"Hey, is that your boyfriend?"

I looked up from the 99-cent record bin and glanced around. There was nobody behind me. The record store clerk was grinning down at me from behind the stack of records we had just brought in.

"Are you talking to me?"

"Yeah. I was asking if that guy's your boyfriend." He nodded toward Travis, who was browsing the CDs at the back of the store.

"Him? No, he's my mom's boyfriend."

"You're pulling my leg. How old's your mom?"

"Why, you wanna date her, too?"

"No, no." He laughed. "You're right. None of my beeswax. Where're you from, anyway?" He leaned forward on his stool, folding his arms on the counter.

"Rivington Street." I turned back to the bin I was looking through. The store reminded me of a place called Rocksteady Records back home. Except this place had even more weird old records. Like Ethel Merman's disco album. I thought about buying that one to send to Dory, as a joke.

"You don't sound like you're from Rivington Street," the kid behind the counter kept on. He was annoyingly chipper, a chubby teddy bear in a Black Flag T-shirt.

"I was born here. But I just moved back. I've been living in South Carolina since I was two."

"Oh yeah? Whereabouts?" He took the record off the player next to the cash register, and the store got strangely quiet.

"You wouldn't know it," I mumbled.

"Try me." He slipped one of my mom's records out of its sleeve and put it on the turntable.

"Millville. It's south of—"

"Spartanburg. Right off 85. I'm from Gaffney, myself." He dropped the needle on the record, and the sound of twangy, buzzing guitars filled the shop.

"No way."

"I can see the big peach from my mom's backyard," he said. Gaffney was famous for its huge water tower in the shape of a peach.

"Really?"

"Naw, I'm from Pickens. I just say I'm from Gaffney to impress the ladies."

I rolled my eyes. He moved the stack of records aside and extended his hand.

"I'm Gram Medley. Spelled G-R-A-M, as in Parsons. My mom's favorite singer." We shook hands. I noticed how nice his smile was.

"Maria Costello."

"As in Elvis?"

"I guess."

"So what brings you to Rivington Street, Maria Costello?"

"School."

"Same here. I'm at NYU, myself. Music major. I play piano. Tried to get into Juilliard, but"—he shrugged—"turns out genius in Gaffney is only fair to middlin' at Juilliard."

"Travis is a musician, too," I blurted out. I wanted to steer the conversation away from school. I wasn't sure why, but suddenly I didn't want Gram to know that I was only in eleventh grade. "He's a guitarist."

"Oh yeah? Where's he from?"

"Um . . . Queens, I think."

"That's too bad." He reached into his back pocket. "We have these parties, me and my roommates over at NYU. SSKs." He pulled a flyer out of his pocket and handed it to me. It was the size of a postcard and read SSK POTLUCK—EVERY THIRD THURSDAY. SUITE 230, HARRISON HALL. SWEET TEA PROVIDED—BYOB.

"SSKs?"

"Smart Southern Kids. My roommate Sandy came up with it. I wanted to call it Rednecks Who Read, but he's a physics major and I guess he didn't want it to sound like a book club.

It's all us Southern kids who are at NYU. Everybody makes food—fried okra, fried chicken, turnip greens—then we just eat, hang out, talk about all the stuff we miss from back home. We meet up every third Thursday and on certain special occasions, like the Alabama-Auburn game. Or Clemson-Carolina." He gave me a knowing smile, but I'd spent years not giving a crap who won the stupid Clemson-Carolina football game.

"Sounds like fun."

"It is—wait, hand it back for a second." I gave the card to him, and he scribbled something on the other side.

"My phone number." He handed it back to me. "Give me a call if you wanna come down to the next meet-up. Or if you just wanna talk or whatever."

"Thanks." I could feel myself blushing. How did this happen? All of a sudden some college guy was giving me his number. What do I do now?

"Hey, I thought I heard my name." Travis leaned on the counter.

"Maria was just telling me you're from Queens. Hey, I'm Gram." Gram reached his hand down to Travis. Travis didn't take it. Gram cleared his throat.

"Gram's from Gaffney. Near where I live. Used to live," I explained to Travis. Travis just looked at me, then glared back at Gram.

"Well, uh—y'all sure are getting rid of some good records here," Gram said, holding up the cover of the record he was playing. "You really wanna part with this Moby Grape? And this live Neil Young record—it's not out on CD—"

"Yeah, we're sure," Travis said quickly. "So, what can you do?"

"Lessee, I can give you . . ." Gram flipped through the stack, counting quietly under his breath. "Eighty-five. Sound fair?"

"You can't do a hundred?"

"Standard price we pay is two bucks a record. A few of these are worth a little more than that, so"—he shrugged, apologetic— "I'm actually rounding up."

"Ninety, man. You said yourself, we're getting rid of some good stuff." Travis gave him a look. "Ninety's fair."

Gram looked at me, shaking his head. "Ninety it is, then," he muttered, opening the cash register. "Dang. My boss is gonna kill me." He counted out ninety dollars. "Here you go." Travis pocketed the wad of cash.

"Thanks," I said.

"Pleasure doing business with you." Gram smiled at me. If he was upset over Travis haggling for more money, he was over it already.

"Maria, I got rehearsal." Travis was already at the door. "We better go." He didn't even wait for me; he just left. The bell on the door handle clanked, and I had to hurry to catch up.

"Nice meeting you," I called back to Gram.

"Likewise!" I heard him shout as the door shut behind me.

"Hey! Slow down!" I had to run to catch up to Travis. "We're not that late. What's the matter?"

"That guy's a scumbag."

"You know him?"

"No, but I could tell by looking at him. Some fatass in a Black Flag T-shirt playing hippie music. He's a poser."

"I thought he was nice. He gave you ninety bucks. And he invited me to a party." I showed Travis the flyer.

"Gram. What's he do, deal drugs?"

"He's named after Gram . . . Parton or something."

"What's SSK mean? Is that some kinda skinhead thing?" He flipped the flyer back at me and took his cigarette pack out of his pocket.

"No, it stands for Smart Southern Kids."

"SSKs," he grunted. "You sure it's not some racist deal?"

"No, it's a potluck." I shoved the card back into my pocket. "At least, I don't think it's racist. Just because it's Southern doesn't mean—"

"And he's way too old for you," Travis interrupted, lighting his cigarette.

"Look who's talking."

"That's different." He exhaled smoke. "Stay away from that guy."

"Okay, *Dad*." I gave a fake army salute.

"Whatever." We stopped at the corner for the Don't Walk sign.

"One of these days. To the moon!" I put on my gruff businessman voice again and nudged him with my elbow. He didn't laugh, but I could see, as he turned to watch the traffic, the edges of his lips lifting into a smile.

I was running in a dream. Running through the streets, dodging cabs, trying to get to school on time. I could hear my mother, but I couldn't see her. Her words turned into yelps and moans, something that sounded like "Move! Move!" I ran as hard as I could, but the blocks were endless. The harder I ran, the slower I moved. Finally I woke up, sweating, tangled in the sheets. My mom was on the floor at the foot of the bed. In the fuzzy dark, I could see her sitting cross-legged by the faint orange glow of the stereo light. The music played quietly, the same woman's voice I'd heard in my dream.

"I was afraid I might wake you up," Mom said.

"It's all right. I was having a dream. Are you okay?"

"Yeah. I couldn't sleep. I kinda needed to hear this." She held up a record cover I couldn't quite see. I moved to sit at the end of the bed. She lit a cigarette.

"*Radio Ethiopia.* Maybe my favorite record of all time. I think it's even better than *Raw Power* or *Let It Bleed* or *Highway 61* or even the first Ramones record." She handed the cover to me. It was silver and black. Patti Smith. The same woman from the other record, the one she'd wanted me to listen to that first night I moved in.

"The first time I heard this, I knew I had to get out of New Jersey. This is where it was all happening. Andy Warhol, the whole scene. New York was where the artists lived, and that's all I ever wanted to be." She leaned her head back against the foot of my bed. "The first night I lived here, it was the night of the blackout. Summer of '77. You know about the blackout?"

"No."

"God, the whole city lost its freakin' mind. It was, like, a hundred degrees. Power went out everywhere. My friend Jaina and I went out to celebrate my arrival. We were walking over to Lee's place, and all of a sudden the streetlamps went out. It was pitch-black—no lights in the windows, nothing. That was the night I met your father. He pulled us into this club where he was working and made us stay there until he could take us home. We should've been scared, but we didn't know until the next morning about the looting and the fires, how bad it was. There were all these candles, and somebody had a battery-operated tape player or eight-track or something. I just remember we kept listening to this one guy's tape of, like, the soundtrack to *Superfly*. We were all drinking wine and dancing our asses off. Your dad and I didn't start going out till later, but we became friends that night. It's so hard to believe—" Her voice broke. She took a drag on her cigarette. I watched the orange tip glow brighter for a moment, then fade.

"I mean, back then it was like I was trying to see everything. I went to museums; I studied every brushstroke of every painting until I knew it by heart. I knew it was important, but it felt like school, you know? Music—rock and roll—that was lifeblood. Pure energy. I heard these records—I heard Patti—and I felt . . . electrified or something. Like I could paint for days. I realized it's all one thing: music, painting—it's all art. It's all—" She stopped. "I never made it happen, though, did I? I just didn't have enough time. There's so much more I wanted to do. So much work. I'll never finish it all."

"I'll help you," I said. "We both will. Me and Travis. We've almost got everything packed up, anyway."

"Geez, kid." Her voice broke again. Was she crying? "I didn't mean—" She stopped and kind of laughed. She exhaled. "Sorry. It's just too much."

"It's okay. Maybe it'll be nice over there. In Brooklyn."

"Yeah. I bet Brooklyn's *great*."

She laughed and sniffled, and then she was quiet. My head was still hazy with sleep. I didn't know what to say to fix things, to make her feel better. To let her know that I really could help. So we both just sat there, listening to the record play. It sounded like two women's voices now, braiding and intertwining with a spiky-sounding guitar and a spacy-sounding piano. *I want to feel you in my radio.*

"You know what's weird?" Mom cleared her throat. "*Horses* is the really great one, if you listen to the critics. But this is the one that really blew my mind. I learned everything from Patti. From these records. From what she wrote. I learned about all the great artists and writers, just from reading her interviews in *Creem* magazine when I was a kid. I learned about Brancusi and Modigliani and Jackson Pollock. She'd talk about poets like Baudelaire and Rimbaud the same as Bob Dylan or the Stones, and I realized, you know, art wasn't just this old, done thing. It was new and alive and possible. But mostly it was just her. Patti. She was from New Jersey, like me. And whenever my stepmother would say, 'You gotta stop pissing your life away painting pictures, you're never gonna amount to shit, you gotta learn a trade, go to beauty school or be a secretary,' I'd just think about Patti, and I knew she was wrong.

"I wish you could've been here back then. It was so exciting. It was like, every day there was something new going on. Some new band, some amazing new thing. Every single day. And I felt so open, like . . ." She stopped again. "I don't know. I had all the energy in the world. I was ready for it. But it got so fucking *hard*—"

I heard her inhale, the end of her cigarette glowing brighter again.

"Hard to paint?"

"No. Not hard to paint. Just hard to . . ." Her voice was so quiet I could barely hear her. "Hard to create so much and realize that nobody gave a damn."

The song was slowing down, the voices untwining, whispering back to one. My mother laughed. One of those laughs where you know nothing's really funny.

"Ahh, fuck it," she said. "I should've just started a rock and roll band."

I wanted to tell her that it didn't matter, that I knew she was an artist, that just because she wasn't rich and famous didn't mean she wasn't good. But she sat up suddenly and took the needle off the record. I could hear the tapping of the hot water pipes, and Travis snoring quietly in the other room.

"Sorry," she apologized again. "I can't hear 'Pissing in a River' right now. *Way* too much." She stubbed out her cigarette and stood up. "And I'm keeping you awake."

"It's okay," I said. "I like talking about music and books and everything."

"Then we'll talk more later on." She ruffled my hair and turned the stereo off. The orange glow went away. It was completely dark.

"Can you see?" I asked, climbing back into bed.

"Yeah. I know this place by heart."

The next morning, when I woke up, I remembered my mom playing her records in the dark. I wondered if I'd dreamed it all. But then, when I went to grab my backpack on the way out the door, I noticed a stack of books balanced on Travis's amp, tied with a burgundy ribbon. On top was one of Mom's notes, written in silver ink on a black note card.

Maria,
Here's your real New York education!
Start with *Cowboy Mouth* and work your
way down. Side two of *Radio Ethiopia*
coming soon...
V.

I untied the ribbon and looked at them all. The creased covers, the edges of the pages worn soft from my mother's hands turning them over and over again. I ran my finger along the titles, the names. Sam Shepard. Patti Smith. *Babel. Faithfull. Edie.* Jim Carroll. Arthur Rimbaud. Charles Baudelaire. *The True Adventures of the Rolling Stones.*

I tucked the first three into my already-stuffed backpack and ran out the door.

I was sitting there in chemistry class, thinking about everything but chemistry. I was thinking about my mom in the blackout in 1977. I was thinking about Patti Smith. I was thinking about Gram, the kid from the record store, who I had decided was not annoying at all but was pretty nice. I was wishing he went to Prince Academy, or that I went to NYU.

"Hey, Beverly. Bev-er-*leee* . . ." The guy behind me was chanting. I had my nose in my book, trying to speed-read the last of the chapter that I was supposed to have read on the subway that morning, when I was reading *Cowboy Mouth* instead.

"Beverly!" The guy yanked my hair. I turned around. What was his name? Tyler. He was in my homeroom, too. And he was a smartass.

"Are you talking to me?"

"Yeah, I'm talking to you, Bev!"

"My name's not Beverly," I told him. "It's Maria."

"Right. Listen, Beverly," the kid went on. "I was wondering if you could possibly go sit somewhere else or at least move your big head over so us normal-sized people back here can maybe see a *little* of the chalkboard?" The kids next to him laughed. "I mean, if it's not too much to ask, Beverly."

"I told you, my name's Maria." I gritted my teeth.

"Beverly, it's *very* simple." He folded his arms. "But I'll explain it slowly so that even you can understand. We call you Beverly, Beverly, because you're a hillbilly. Get it now? *Beverly Hillbilly.*"

Half the class was cracking up. I could feel my face getting hot. One kid made twangy banjo noises, like the song from that movie *Deliverance*.

"Is that how you got so freakishly tall, Beverly?" Tyler asked. "Your mom sleep with her cousin or something?"

I was afraid I was about to cry. But I didn't. I took a deep breath and flipped him the bird instead.

"How d'you like this view, Tyler?" I asked. The kids at his table went "Oooh," but I grabbed my books and got up before he could say anything else. My eyes were so full of tears, I almost smacked right into Mr. Lehrman, our teacher, as I was walking out the door.

"Everything all right, uh—" He paused. Trying to remember my name.

"I feel sick," I muttered, and walked out the door, down the hall, to my locker, to the front door, and out of there, out into the street.

* * *

We said good-bye to the apartment on Rivington Street early that Saturday morning and drove over the river, to Brooklyn. Travis and his friend Slade, the bass player, took turns carrying boxes up from the truck while Mom and I stayed in the apartment, cleaning it up and unpacking boxes. The new apartment had a bigger kitchen, but otherwise it was pretty much the same as the last one. One bedroom, so I ended up on the futon in the living room again. And no more claw-foot tub. At least it was only one flight up.

"I can't believe we're going to have to hear that music all night long," she said above the rough thump of techno coming from the strip club downstairs. "I don't want to see you anywhere near that place, you understand?" She waggled a bunch of hangers at me.

"Yes, ma'am." I handed her some clothes. "Why would I go into a strip club, anyway?"

"I don't know. Just don't. And don't call me ma'am, either. I'm not that old."

"Yes, sir."

She threw a sweater at me. I threw it back.

"Everybody's a comedian." She hung up the sweater. "Oh, no."

"What?"

"There's a tear in my jacket." She held up a black blazer. "A rip in the sleeve. Right there."

"It's right on the seam. No big deal." I looked at it. "I can sew it up for you. I fix Dad's clothes all the time."

"You do?"

"Sure."

"Well, aren't you helpful." She handed me the blazer. "This

isn't just any jacket, though. Wait right there—I'll show you." She wound her way through the maze of boxes to the living room, where she dug through the records she'd already unpacked. The stereo was the first thing we set up, so we'd have something to listen to while we worked.

"Here it is. Look." She came back to the bedroom holding the same Patti Smith record she'd given me the first night I'd come to New York. The one with the black-and-white cover.

"It's the same one," she said, pointing to the jacket Patti had slung over her shoulder.

"The jacket?"

"*The* jacket. This is Patti's." She took the ripped blazer out of my hands and held it up. "You wanna try it on?"

"Okay." I shrugged and slid my arms into the sleeves.

"Oh my gosh." My mom sort of gasped. "It fits you perfectly."

"It's nice." It was a better fit than my school blazer. Almost like it had been tailored for me.

"I knew this painter named Ellen, and she lived at the Chelsea Hotel the same time that Patti did," Mom explained. "She went into her place after she moved out—Patti's place, I mean—and she found this hanging in the back of the closet. It was right after *Horses* came out, and the cover was so famous. Ellen couldn't believe she left it. But she gave it to me because she knew how much I totally love Patti. Didn't you just love this record?"

"Um, it was okay."

"Okay? Maria! Nobody thinks *Horses* is *okay*. You either freak out and love it or you don't."

"I guess I—I didn't really listen to it. All the way through." I busied myself studying the record cover. I wasn't so sure the jacket I had on was the one from the picture. And I wasn't so sure I wanted to hear more of this music. I thought about the night I woke up to my mom listening to that Patti Smith album in the dark. It seemed to make her so sad.

"I knew you didn't listen to this record! Because you'd totally flip out if you heard it. Come on, let's go put it on right now."

I took Mom's jacket off as carefully as I could, trying not to rip the sleeve any more. Maybe my mom had already forgotten that night. Or maybe this record didn't make her as sad. She climbed through the boxes again, back to the living room, where the turntable sat on the bare floor. She took off the Talking Heads and put the Patti Smith record on. That line was playing right when I walked in. *Jesus died for somebody's sins but not mine.*

"Oh my God, we should totally smoke a joint right now," my mom said. "This record is even more amazing when you're—" She stopped and put a finger to her lips. "I shouldn't have said that, should I?"

"It's okay," I said. I didn't care if my mom smoked pot. Even though I knew it was bad for me, and I could've gotten into major trouble, I smoked pot sometimes when my dad was gone and I was home alone and scared. I guess I figured I could be doing a lot worse.

"No, it's so not okay!" She covered her eyes with her hands. "I'm trying to be a good mom, I really am." She ran her fingers through her hair. "I completely suck at it."

"You don't suck. Come on," I told her. "You're, like, the coolest mom ever."

"But I don't know where to draw the line, you know? I feel

like I should be looking after you more, going to your school and meeting your teachers and all that PTA-mom stuff. But then I think back to when I was your age, and I hated how my stepmother tried to run my life. It sucked. And you're so, like, Super Kid anyway—"

"I'm definitely not super." I laughed.

"But you totally are! I was such a basket case when I was your age. And I look at you, at how grown-up you are and how you just— I mean, look at how you moved up here and started this school, getting up early, studying so hard. I'm so incredibly proud of you right now and I know that I—" She cleared her throat. She sounded almost like she was going to cry. "I know it doesn't have anything to do with me. I mean, I feel bad that I wasn't there when you were growing up, but if I had been, then maybe you'd be a basket case like I was."

She got up and went to the kitchen counter, where a pack of cigarettes and a lighter sat next to a stack of dishes wrapped in newspaper. She shook one of the cigarettes out of the pack and lit it.

"How awesome is this song, right?" She waved her cigarette in the air, smiling. "Didn't I tell you Patti's the greatest?"

"Yeah. This is pretty great," I said quietly.

"I wish I could've seen you more. When you were growing up. I know I should've—I don't know, I should've tried harder. It seemed like I never had enough money to get down there, and your dad was always working." She took a long drag on the cigarette. "I still feel guilty that I left in the first place. But I wouldn't have— I just couldn't deal with the—" She shook her head. "I couldn't deal with South Carolina. It was like Jersey but worse. Like, dead. Just a totally dead place, dead people.

Nobody had any ideas. Any life. Just nothing happening at all. You know what I mean?"

"Yeah." I knew exactly what she meant. But she was kind of freaking me out. There was a strange, serious look in her eyes, and she seemed nervous.

"Okay, where do you want this?" Travis stood in the doorway with Slade, each of them holding opposite ends of a huge canvas marked with broad, curving brushstrokes of purple and black.

"In the bedroom. Wait, who's watching the truck?" Mom asked.

"Some kid we gave a dollar to."

"Oh my gosh, Travis, please tell me you didn't."

"Vic, he's, like, ten."

"Yeah, so he's probably taken everything but the rearview mirror!" Mom went running off down the stairs, her cigarette trailing smoke and ash, while Travis and Slade moved the painting into the bedroom, grunting and laughing at the whole thing.

I was in the middle of leaving my dad a message when he picked up the phone.

"Maria? What's wrong? Is everything okay?"

"It's fine, Dad. Hi."

"How's everything going up there?"

"It's okay," I said. "It's great. I really like the school. I was just calling because we—well, because we moved."

"You moved? What happened?"

"Nothing happened. They were just selling Mom's building, so we got a cheaper place out in Brooklyn."

"*Brooklyn?* Jesus, Maria, is it safe? What's the neighborhood like?"

"It's like a . . ." I figured I'd better not mention the strip club. "I dunno, it's just a regular neighborhood. It's near the, um, the BQE? We just moved in today. I wanted to call and give you the new phone number and address."

"All right. Hang on." There was silence on the line. "Let me find a pen."

My dad and I got along a lot better when I was little. I was too young to understand why my mom left, but I was young enough to accept that this was how it was, just my dad and me. And for a long time, that was fine. We always did things together on the weekends, went camping or played catch or built things together in the garage. Little projects out of scrap wood, like jewelry boxes or doll beds. He had girlfriends from time to time. I never got close to any of them, but I never hated them or felt jealous, either. I kind of suspected that he never really got over my mom, because my dad's a nice guy and not too bad looking, but none of the women he dated ever stuck around.

Over the last couple of years, though, things changed. I guess it always changes when you grow up and lose interest in doll beds and playing catch. But without a mom to be our go-between, we became more like roommates than family. He had always worked nights, waking up just after I got home from school and having his breakfast when I was having dinner. Coming home in time to have his dinner while I ate breakfast. But the house needed repairs, and we needed money. He'd always been weird about asking my grandmother for it, even though she's loaded. So a few years ago, he started taking on extra shifts. I barely saw him during the week, and he spent the weekends fixing the foundation or putting on our new roof. We communicated via little notes, mostly from him. Asking me to do chores, leaving a blank check and a grocery list, pinning notes to work shirts so I'd mend the rips and tears.

I felt like a total slave, and I knew it was all going to come to a head sooner or later. At first, hanging out with Brian and the guys helped. I liked staying out half the night, sneaking out after Dad left. But it was a mistake in the end. I can see that now. I just don't know why I couldn't make my dad see it like I did. I knew he was there. I saw evidence of him in the piles of dirty laundry, the dishes in the sink. And I know he must've seen evidence of me, too. Evidence in the neat pyramids of folded socks left on his dresser, the stocked fridge, the neatly swept floors. But in the end, I don't think he really saw me, any more than I saw him. Which is to say, we had pulled off this amazing feat: We both managed to become completely invisible.

5

"Hey, Beverly, it's your lucky day."

I looked up. Tyler was standing by my table in the cafeteria, him and his buddies.

"What do you want?" I looked up warily. I was minding my own business, reading one of my mom's books. *Faithfull*, the one about Mick Jagger's girlfriend, Marianne Faithfull. I was right at the part where she was kicking her drug habit and making *Broken English*, her big comeback album. My mom had just played it for me last night, and I still had the music in my head.

"We couldn't help but notice you're all alone here, so we brought you a friend. Beverly, meet Pus Bomb." Tyler shoved this kid Eric Nussbaum toward me. I'd seen Eric around. He was a scrawny underclassman with Tourette's Syndrome. Everyone made fun of the poor guy, even though he didn't go around yelling obscenities, like people always joke about. He was just twitchy, and he stuttered a little. Tyler had him by the neck.

"Tyler, leave him alone."

"No, no, Beverly. We were thinking about it, and we feel really bad that you haven't made any friends here at Prince. So we racked our brains, and we came up with this brilliant idea. You and Pus Bomb, here. I think you'd make a lovely couple."

"I don't think my social life is any of your business," I said.

"Oh, but look at the two of you together. Pus Bomb, have a seat next to Beverly." Tyler shoved him, and Eric fell into the seat next to me. He tried to grab the table to steady himself as he fell, and his hand landed right in my Jell-O. The poor kid was shaking and twitching all over. I handed him a napkin.

"Look, guys." Tyler nudged his two buddies. "I'm having a vision. I can see it all now—prom king and queen! Here they are!" He held his hands up like a movie director framing a shot.

"All right, that's enough," I muttered. "Can I please finish my—"

"Hey, everybody!" Tyler yelled across the whole cafeteria. "I nominate Pus Bomb and Beverly for prom king and—"

"God*dam* it, that's enough!" I stood up and yelled, not realizing how loud I was or what I'd said. I'd slammed my tray down on the table, too, and now there was Jell-O and mashed potatoes splattered all over—on the table, on Eric's sleeve, on Mom's book. The whole cafeteria got quiet. One of the teachers was walking over to us, stern and serious.

"Okay, don't get all excited." Tyler laughed, holding up his hands. "It's just a joke, Bev."

"What's going on over here?" The teacher put his hands on his hips. I didn't know who he was.

"Nothing, Mr. Asher. We were just joking around." Tyler

slouched, his hands in his pockets. "I guess Maria took it kind of seriously. Sorry, sir."

"Tyler, you boys go back to your seats." Mr. Asher turned to me and Eric. Tyler and his friends slunk off.

"You're new, correct?" The teacher was talking to me like I was the troublemaker.

"Yes, sir," I said.

"We don't appreciate those kind of vulgar outbursts here at Prince. This isn't public school, miss. Please behave yourself in the future."

I was too stunned to say anything. This guy Asher was pretty much taking Tyler's side. He gave me a serious staredown, then turned and went back to his seat. I wiped Jell-O off Mom's book with a napkin, keeping my head down so that Eric wouldn't see that I was about to cry.

"Sorry," he said softly.

"It's not your fault," I told him. "Does it get any better around here?"

"I'm af-afraid not," Eric whispered. He got up and went back to his table. I tucked the book under my arm and took my tray back to the tray station. I walked out of the cafeteria, and for the second time in two weeks, I got my jacket and backpack out of my locker and walked out the front door without telling anyone where I was going. Because I didn't really know, myself.

I felt like walking for a while, even though I didn't know where. I put Supergirl Mixtape #8 in my Walkman, one of the ones with all the pissed-off-sounding PJ Harvey songs on it, and decided I'd just walk around until I didn't feel like screaming and throwing things anymore.

The only problem was, the Upper East Side wasn't a very angry place to walk around. It wasn't like downtown, with all the punks and bums and music and sidewalks full of bootlegs and books. It was cleaner and quieter. I mostly saw old people and delivery boys, moms with strollers, and dressed-up women walking their equally well-dressed tiny poodles and dachshunds. The stores were all nice boutiques, fancy places with fancy clothes and expensive sunglasses and purses, instead of used records and vintage shoes and Tibetan knickknacks. It didn't really matter, though. I was glad to be walking around in the gray October chill instead of sitting in class at Prince, taking abuse from that idiot Tyler and his friends.

I stopped at a Don't Walk sign when I felt a hand on my shoulder. I must've jumped a mile. I figured it was somebody from Prince, or else I was getting mugged. But when I turned around, I saw the woman from the apartment that day. My mother's landlord. Her boss. Nina. I took off my headphones.

"Maria? Sorry, I didn't mean to startle you," she said. "I called your name, but you didn't hear me. I'm Nina. We met at your mother's apartment."

"Yeah. Yes, ma'am. I remember."

"I trust you're not truant."

"What?"

"Skipping school."

"Oh. Oh, no, we had a sub. And my last period's study hall, anyway, so . . ." I trailed off, shocked at how quickly I'd come up with a lie. "I'm just—" I looked up, suddenly realizing that I wasn't sure where I was, or how to get to my train stop on Lexington. "I'm just taking a walk," I said finally.

"As long as you're in the neighborhood, can I interest you in a cup of tea?"

"Tea?" I was all out of lies. I felt like Nina was the enemy, but I couldn't think of a good reason not to go with her.

"Tea sounds nice."

Nina lifted the teabag delicately out of her cup and set it on the plain white saucer. Almost everything in the restaurant was white. The walls were decorated with slender silver bud vases, sprigs of willow branching against the plaster.

"I feel I should apologize to you," Nina said.

"Apologize to me? For what?"

"The apartment over Citygirls—it's not the most scenic locale. When my husband died, I swore I would sell that place. But as it turns out, of all his real-estate investments, Citygirls is the most profitable. Embarrassing, but profitable." Nina smiled as she sipped her tea. "At any rate, it's only temporary. I'm working on finding Victoria a more suitable apartment. A girl your age should have a room of her own, don't you think?"

"I guess," I replied. I didn't mind the futon that much.

"So, how do you like Prince Academy?" Nina asked.

"It's all right." I gulped my tea. It tasted sharp. Tart. Green ginger lotus blossom. Nina's recommendation. I could feel her watching me. "I mean, it could be worse."

"That's hardly a ringing endorsement," she commented.

"Sorry. I know it's your husband's school and all." I paused, wondering how a guy who went to Prince Academy ended up owning a strip club. I almost smiled, imagining Tyler's future career. "But it sucks at Prince. The kids are stuck-up jerks and the teachers are just as bad."

"I was afraid you'd say that. Prince has a reputation for being rather stuffy, but it was the only school of its caliber that we could get you into on such short notice, and without taking entrance exams. It didn't hurt that my husband left Prince Academy a sizable donation in his will." Nina gave a tight-lipped smile. "I hope you won't let it get in the way of our friendship."

"Our—wait a sec. *You* got me into Prince?"

"Your grandmother and I did, yes."

"Okay, I'm confused. How is it that you're friends with my grandmother and my mom at the same time? They hate each other."

"Don't they!" Nina laughed. "I am only an acquaintance of your grandmother's. We've actually never met in person. I am your mother's patron. Rather, I *was* your mother's patron, when she was still a practicing artist."

"She's still practicing," I said quickly, in my mother's defense.

"She is?"

"Yeah. I mean . . ." I swallowed, not sure where I was going with this. "She's always drawing. Little sketches. She draws all the time."

"Sketches." Nina sighed. "When I first saw your mother's work—completely by accident, by the way—she lived in a building my husband was buying—I didn't know much about art. But I knew right away, this young woman is a talent. I bought two of her pieces myself that very day, and I persuaded a friend of mine to buy another. But then she just . . . stopped working. And one can't promote an artist who doesn't make any art."

"I guess not," I said. "Why did she stop? Because of my dad?"

"No, although she did seem to hit a creative wall when your father moved you all to the South. I think she was overwhelmed. Fish out of water. That was when I got to know your grandmother. She seems like a lovely woman."

"She's all right."

"Your mother came up with this grand plan to study art at Pratt. Your grandmother offered to pay—she's a big believer in education, as you know. She thought it would help your mother grow up a little, learn some discipline. I became involved simply because I owned paintings that your mother wanted to submit in her portfolio. The next thing I knew, I was helping her enroll, finding her an apartment. Or, rather, I was finding your grandmother the apartment, since it was, after all, her name on the check."

"So this must be déjà vu all over again," I murmured.

"Something like that." Nina laughed. "I maintained a friendship with Victoria—I feel responsible for her, in a way. After she dropped out of school, your grandmother withdrew her support. I persuaded your mother to return to South Carolina— I even bought her a train ticket. But that didn't last. Do you remember any of that, or were you too young?"

"No, I—I wasn't too young," I said. "I remember."

"When she came back to New York, I helped her move to the apartment on Rivington Street, and I tried to look after her. Keep her out of trouble. We all thought she would . . . get it out of her system, somehow. Your grandmother and I. We tried to arrange for you to visit your mother on an earlier occasion—I believe you were thirteen?"

"You did?"

"Your grandmother called me, out of the blue. She said you were quite insistent about wanting to spend time with your mother, and why not? What girl doesn't need her mother at that age? Unfortunately, Victoria was going through one of her more erratic phases. Your grandmother and I discussed bringing you here anyway, almost as a—" Nina paused, thinking.

"Your grandmother had this idea that if you could see your mother behaving irresponsibly, you would realize how lucky you were to live under your father's roof. But I dissuaded her. Thirteen is simply too young to be left alone in a strange city with a mother who was prone to disappearing for weeks at a time."

"You were—" I had a hard time getting my mind around this. How was it that this woman I had never met was making decisions about my life? "Where did she go?"

"Excuse me?"

"Where did she—" I cleared my throat. "Where did my mom go, when she disappeared all the time?"

"That's for you and your mother to discuss. At any rate, when you had your . . . incident, your grandmother called me and asked if I would act as liaison again. When we discussed your mother, we thought it was a better time—maybe the best time—for the two of you—" Nina was interrupted by an electronic chirp. She reached into her purse to silence her beeper, frowning into its glowing digital display.

"Maria, I apologize. Would you excuse me?"

"Sure." I drank the rest of my tea in one gulp. How could I have never known any of this? No wonder my grandmother was so upset with my mom—she thought she was paying for her to go back to school, but she was really just helping her leave my dad. And why now? Why would Nina and my grandmother agree that it was okay for me to come live with my mom, only to have Nina sell the apartment building out from under her? And who was Nina to decide anything about me and my mom, anyway?

"I'm terribly sorry, but there's a slight emergency and I'm going to have to go." Nina was rushing now, taking money out of her purse and handing it to me. "Please, stay and enjoy your tea. Order anything else you like. It was lovely to see you again. I'm sorry that you're having a hard time at Prince, but it'll pass. You're a very bright girl." Nina shook my hand. "And I'm glad you got over your . . . difficulties. I'm glad you're feeling better."

"Thanks," I said as she left. *My difficulties.* I couldn't think of anything else to say. I looked down at the money she'd given me. A twenty-dollar bill. I paid for the two cups of tea and pocketed the rest.

Dory burst into the spare bedroom at my grandmother's without even knocking.

"Is it true?" She was out of breath. She must've run all the way. I was lying on the bed, listening to my grandmother and my father and the psychiatrist and Dory's parents and the phone ringing through the wall. I sat up slowly.

"I thought you were in school," I said. My voice felt ancient. Rusted out from lack of use.

"I was! Maria!" Dory was on the verge of tears. "They said you tried to kill yourself!"

"I wasn't trying to kill myself," I told her. "My father overreacted."

"He *overreacted*? I think I'd overreact, too, if I walked in on my kid slitting her wrists—"

"I wasn't slitting my wrists."

"Show me," Dory demanded.

"Show you what?"

"Your arms. Show me you weren't trying to kill yourself."

"Leave me alone." I lay back down. Dory grabbed my hands and jerked me up. She shoved my sleeves to my elbows.

"Jesus Christ." She inhaled, sucking air through her teeth. "Maria. What have you done?"

"Nothing." I tried to pull away from Dory's grip.

"That's a fucking gory idea of nothing."

I looked down at my arms. I guess seeing the whole thing like that, all of a sudden, it did look pretty shocking. All those ordered little lines, cut in neat rows all up and down my forearms. The first ones had already faded to smooth white scars. But the more recent ones, the ones near my wrists, the ones my dad freaked out over, those were still fresh. Still angry red and bright pink. I saw them like Dory might. Like they were on someone else's skin. Gaping and vulnerable, violent and worrisome as a baby's screaming mouth.

"Why on earth would you do this to yourself?" Dory asked.

"I don't know." I remembered the adrenaline rush that came with each of those neat little lines. The rush that was gone now. What was it that I was trying to feel?

"All this over some stupid guy—"

"It's not just about him."

"Are you on drugs?"

"No."

"What's going on, then?"

"I don't know."

"Damn it, Maria. Something's the matter! Why can't you just—why didn't you call me? You know you can always call me if something's wrong."

"I did." Dory was the first one I called, after everything really fell apart. After that last party, with Brian. "I guess your roommate didn't give you the message. You never called back."

Dory lowered her head. Tears fell from her eyes, blotching the bedspread.

"I'm so sorry," she said. "I should've realized. I should've been there—"

"Don't worry about it." I patted her head, absolving her. "Nobody's ever there."

"Don't say that." Dory looked up at me. "We love you. Your dad loves you. Your grandmother loves you. They're downstairs right now trying to get you into some school in New York. They talked to your mom, and she said you could stay with her. Isn't that what you always wanted? They're bending over backward to make you happy."

"I know."

"So how can you say nobody's there for you? We're all here now. We're all trying to help you."

"I know." I felt like crying, too, but I couldn't. It was like there was nothing left in my eyes. I didn't know how to tell Dory. How to tell her that something inside me felt finished. It was nice of all of them to try to help me. But it was too late for that now.

* * *

It was the first Friday since I told Brian that I didn't want to see him anymore. I'd spent the entire week at school pretending I had to work in the library at lunch, hiding from him and his friends. But now it was Friday. Brian and the team had just won their second wrestling match of the season. I didn't feel like celebrating. I didn't feel like doing much of anything with Brian or any of those guys. I was sitting in my room, sewing one of my dad's shirts and listening to an R.E.M. song on Supergirl Mixtape #11, when Brian came to my window like he always did. He tapped on the glass, and I opened it and leaned out.

"Hey, Maria, come on, we're going to Duffy's."

"I don't feel like it tonight."

"Maria, we're 2-0. Come on." He lit a cigarette.

"I thought the coach told you guys not to smoke."

"Well, he ain't here now, is he?" Brian exhaled, exasperated. "Maria, will you come *on*? Donnie's waiting and we gotta pick up Ben."

"Why don't you guys go ahead? I'll catch up with you later."

Brian squinted up at me.

"This is because of last week, isn't it?" He ashed his cigarette and scratched his head. "I'll be damned. You really wanna break up with me, don't you?"

"Brian, it's just—"

"Because, I mean, shit, I can get another girlfriend. But you're the one I want." He looked up at me, and for a moment I felt a sort of tenderness for him that I hadn't felt before.

"Brian."

"You can't stay mad at me forever, can you?" He smiled.

And the next thing I knew, I was slipping into my sneakers. But I was shaking.

Duffy was an older kid who played in bands and had his own farmhouse that his grandfather left him in his will. Everybody knew who he was, either from his bands or his parties or because they bought pot from him. He grew it out in the woods behind the house. When we got there that night, the place was packed. There were some kids from Langley, but it was mainly public school kids and older kids, probably from the community college.

Brian and Donald and Ben went off in search of the keg. I was already feeling out of my head. I'd skipped dinner and, between the beer in the truck on the way over and the half a joint I smoked on Duffy's front porch, I was halfway to dizzy. I walked into the living room, where a tall, dreadlocked guy was spinning records. I recognized him from Rocksteady, the record store. I'd bought Dory's Christmas present there last year, an import Nick Cave 45.

"Hey, got any requests?" It took me a second to realize that the DJ was talking to me.

"What?" I had to yell over the music.

"Requests. Got something you wanna hear?"

I was too busy trying to keep standing up. I tried to think of some cool band, something Dory would like.

"I remember you," he said. "Nick Cave, right?"

I nodded. "It's not a Nick Cave kind of party, though. What's that you're playing now?"

"Bad Brains. Hang on." The song was ending. He put his headphones on and switched the record. Mudhoney. I knew them from Dory's tapes.

"So, what do you want to hear?"

I shook my head. I wanted to hear my Supergirl Mixtapes, coming out of the cruddy little boom box in my bedroom. I wanted Bikini Kill and L7 and Veruca Salt and Liz Phair and Hole. I wanted to stop feeling dizzy. I wanted to quit being nervous and afraid and fall asleep till noon and wake up to my dad making me breakfast. But none of that was going to happen, at least not tonight. Tonight, I'd be out till dawn. I'd sleep with one eye open, jumping at every snapping branch. I'd wake up to my dad gone, or up on the roof, patching the holes. I'd choke down another cold bowl of cereal and start the washing machine, then go up to my room and start on my homework. I would stay in my room all day, until Brian came by and it all started again.

"Frances Farmer," I said, swallowing hard.

"What?" The DJ flipped his headphones back again.

" 'Frances Farmer Will Have Her Revenge on Seattle.' " My favorite Nirvana song. I handed him the record. *In Utero*. He nodded and put it on. The Mudhoney song ended, and Kurt's buzzing guitar came out of the speakers. The guitar crashed, crashed into something outside the song. Something in the house. Something crashing.

I looked up and saw kids in the hallway moving, shoving, somebody getting pushed out the front door. A beer bottle smashed on the floor. Two guys were yelling. A girl was shouting and running up the stairs. Whatever it was, some people were running away from it and some were going toward it, trying to find out what was going on.

I saw Donald first, then Brian, both of them being sort of shoved and sort of carried down the hall. Duffy was the one doing the shoving and carrying. I was surprised. I didn't know

Duffy that well, but I knew he was a mellow dude. He was a big guy with a beard that went halfway down his chest, and he always wore the same pair of overalls. And now he was throwing Brian and Donald out of the house.

"I'm serious. Y'all go home or I'm calling the cops," Duffy told them.

"Bullshit, man. Bull *shit*," Donald yelled.

"Get outta my house!" Duffy yelled back.

"Fuck you, Duffy!" Brian turned himself loose from Duffy's grip. "Let gowah me, I gotta find my girlfriend."

"Well, find her and take off, dude." Duffy let him go, and Brian squirmed free. I swallowed hard, remembering that the girlfriend was me. Brian saw me by the turntables and stormed toward me.

"Maria, let's go." He grabbed my arm.

"Ow, Brian—"

"Hey, man, watch it—" the DJ called out to him. As I jerked my hand out of Brian's grip, my arm swung back and knocked hard into the DJ's table, making the record skip and scratch.

"We're getting out of this shithole." Brian glared at me. I took one look at his eyes and knew there was something else going on, something he'd taken besides beer and pot. His pupils were huge. He was pale and sweating. The darkness in his eyes scared me to death.

"I'm not going with you like that," I said.

"Like hell you're not."

The DJ intervened. "Hey, man, maybe you oughta cool out."

"Fuck you! This is none of your fucking business!" Brian roared at him. He grabbed my hand again and this time there was no getting away. "Maria! Goddam it, first you don't wanna come, now you don't wanna leave. Why don't you make up your goddamned simple little mind for once in your pathetic life—"

"I'm not going anywhere with you!" I heard my own voice ring out, high above the music. "I don't ever want to see you again! I'm not your girlfriend, I'm not your friend, and you can say whatever you want about me but you better take your fucking hands off me right now!" I was screaming, shrieking like something out of a cartoon. Some shrill, thinly painted version of myself. But everyone was quiet. Everyone was staring. Brian dropped my hand. I felt the blood rush back into my fingers. He leaned in close to me. The music had stopped. Or maybe I just couldn't hear it anymore. All I could hear was Brian.

"You little bitch," he muttered, his breath hot on my neck. "You stupid little bitch. I'm gonna kill you. You hear me? I know where you live. I'm gonna break your fucking neck."

"All right, kiddies, that's enough." The DJ took me by the shoulders and Duffy pulled Brian toward the door. My hands were shaking again. The next thing I knew, I was in the bathroom with the DJ. I couldn't remember how we got there.

"Are you sure you're okay?" he asked. I nodded. There was still a lot of yelling going on outside.

"That's your boyfriend?"

I shrugged. His voice was so nice. The DJ's. He had this accent—Jamaican or something. I looked up and saw him studying me with this worried look on his face. I started crying and I couldn't stop.

"Hey. Don't cry. It's gonna be all right now. Nothing's going to happen. He's leaving." The DJ tried to reach out to me, to put his arms around me or something. I shook my head, pushing away from him.

"No, no, no—"

"Duffy's throwing him out. We'll get you a ride home. Do you have any other friends here?"

"No."

"Is there somebody I can call for you?"

I thought of Dory, but she was all the way down in Athens. I shook my head. I was still crying.

"Don't worry about it. I'll take you home, all right? Let's just wait until Duffy gets them out of here. How's that?"

I nodded, trying to stop crying.

"I'm Lucas," he said.

"Maria."

Lucas pulled a bunch of toilet paper off the roll and handed it to me. I took it and blew my nose. He put his hand on my shoulder, and I flinched. I was backed up against the bathroom wall, as far into the corner as I could get.

"Hey, relax." He laughed. "Is it because I'm black?"

"No," I shook my head. I tried to smile at him, but I couldn't. I was crying again now, harder than before. I let the DJ—Lucas—take me into his arms and hug me. There was something strange about it, and I realized that I couldn't remember the last time a guy—Brian, my dad, anyone—had hugged me.

"Shh, it's all right now. I'm gonna take care of you. You trust me?" Lucas whispered. I nodded slowly. I wanted to trust him. "I promise, I'm not gonna let any of those guys hurt you."

I let him hug me again. It was nice to lean against him, to

feel his arms around me, patting my back. I finally stopped crying and looked up at him.

"What about the music?" I asked.

"Don't worry about it." He laughed. "I think the party's over."

Mom was curled up on the futon when I got home. She was dressed in her bathrobe, watching a black-and-white movie on TV.

"Hey," I said. "How come you're not at work?"

"I called in sick. I think I'm getting a cold. How was school?"

"Okay, I guess." I took off my Prince blazer, wishing I could burn it.

"Wanna come watch this movie with me? *Stardust Memories.* Classic Woody Allen. It just started, too." She sneezed.

I sat down beside her. "You want me to get you some juice or something?" I asked.

"No, I'm fine. Travis went to get me some NyQuil. I think it's just, you know, all the stress from moving. Oh, look." Mom pointed out a serious-looking brunette on the screen. "Charlotte Rampling. Isn't she gorgeous? I'd kill for cheekbones like that."

"You have excellent cheekbones, Mom," I told her.

"Really?" She smiled, her eyes and nose matching red. I looked at her. My mother. I wanted to tell her that she was beautiful. I wanted to ask her where she went when she disappeared for weeks at a time. I wanted to tell her that I felt the same way sometimes—that I felt like I wanted to just disappear.

But I didn't say any of those things. Instead, I felt angry. I wanted to ask her why Nina had to be our go-between. I wanted to tell her about all these guys, these jerks, Tyler at Prince and Brian back at home. I wanted her to tell me how I was supposed to handle all of this, what I was supposed to do. But I didn't know where to start. All these words, these questions, felt balled-up in my throat, prickling and huge. My eyes teared up, and I started to cry. I looked away, hoping Mom wouldn't notice, but she did.

"Hey, Marinee-beanee, what's wrong?"

"I guess I just sort of . . . had a crappy day."

"Aww. Come here." She pulled me into her arms. It was a relief, somehow. Just to rest there in her arms and cry.

"You wanna talk about it?"

"No." That balled-up thing in my throat could stay where it was. I was afraid to start unraveling it. "Not right now." I stole some of her Kleenex and blew my nose.

"So we'll just sit here and be snotty together. How's that?"

I nodded. I would tell her, eventually. I would ask her all my questions, and she would have the answers. I guess it was some kind of special mom thing. Sitting there next to her, I felt like everything was going to be okay.

"Just watch Charlotte Rampling," she whispered, turning up the sound. "She's a total goddess."

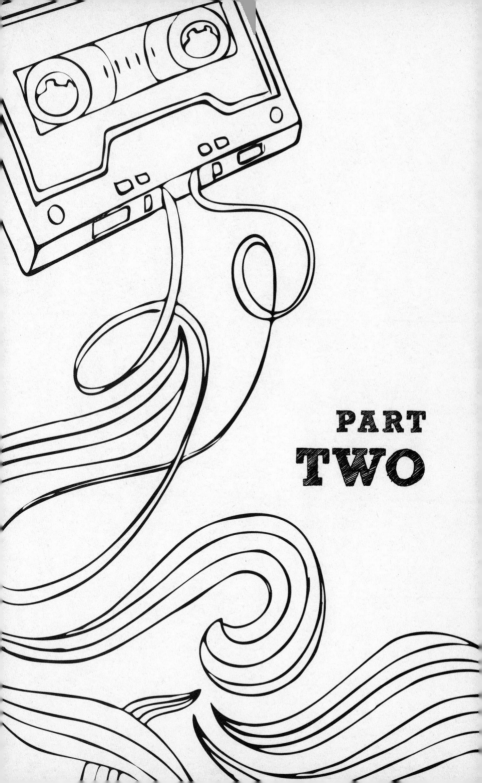

PART TWO

6

It was almost two weeks after the whole cafeteria thing with Tyler that I decided to start skipping school in earnest. I mean, I guess it wasn't that big of a decision. The dread of going to Prince just piled up day after day, until finally the fear of getting caught cutting school was nothing compared to the dread of having to walk through those doors. On the day I finally quit, I stood there outside, watching everybody else go in. I felt a serene calm wash over me as I realized that I wasn't going up those marble steps anymore. Finally I just walked off down the block. Nobody ran after me. Nobody called my name and demanded that I get to class. Nobody chased me down and shook me and told me I'd better turn myself around and march right back there. Nobody even noticed I was gone.

And that was the last time I set foot anywhere near Prince Academy.

I got back on the subway, heading downtown. My heart started beating fast. What was I doing? I'd never been a big fan of school, but at least I'd showed up. Now what was I supposed to do? I couldn't go back to the apartment. But I couldn't just spend the rest of the day riding the subway, either.

I got off at Union Square. Walking around in the cool air felt better. I stood on the corner, waiting for the light to change. The big Virgin Megastore was closed. The movie theater wasn't open yet. The coffee shop on the next block looked busy, though. I decided to go in and wait there for a while, until I came up with a better plan.

After a couple of hours in the coffee shop, eating a bagel and reading Mom's copy of *Edie*, a book about Andy Warhol's main superstar, I got back on the train and headed farther downtown, to find the record store where Travis and I sold Mom's records. The record store where I met Gram. I was glad to see him behind the counter.

"Hey, I know you," he said. "Rivington Street. Don't tell me—Maria?"

"Yeah. Gram, right?"

"You got it. Cold out?"

I nodded. "Getting kinda chilly." The store was warm, but I kept my coat zipped, anyway. I didn't want Gram to see my uniform.

"You got here just in time to hear my namesake." He handed me the album cover. A bunch of guys in sequined suits out in the desert. Country music wailed over the speakers. *This old town's filled with sin, it'll swallow you in.* I handed the album cover back to him.

"You've heard of these guys, right? The Flying Burrito Brothers?" he asked.

"Not really, no."

"Oh, man, it's primo. Of course, I'm biased. But even though Gram Parsons gets all the credit for the whole country-rock thing, there was so much good shit coming out of California back then. Gene Clark from the Byrds. Mike Nesmith from the Monkees. Man, that dude's solo stuff blows my mind. And then you got Neil Young, that whole Doom Trilogy. And, you know, even though people think of the Band as a Woodstock thing, they were out in LA—their entire second album was recorded in Sammy Davis Junior's house!" He chuckled. "Man, I love that shit. But by the time you get to the Eagles, it's pretty much got the life squeezed out of it. You know what I mean?"

"Sure," I said. I had no idea what he meant.

"Then after the Laurel Canyon scene, you got the punk stuff happening, late seventies. Black Flag. The Germs. Fear. X. Man, I love X. You can play me some of that Billy Zoom guitar any day of the *week*. California, man. I tell you what—I've just about had it with New York City. One more winter and I'm done. I'm transferring out to the Golden State. I can't take no more."

"You're leaving the city?" I couldn't believe it. The one nice guy I'd met.

"Uh, well, not right away. It's a big tangle. Money and credits and all that. Tell you the truth, though—I'm thinking about taking some time off from school."

"I've kinda been thinking about the same thing," I told him.

"It's scary though, ain't it? You lose that safety net— whoosh!" He whipped his hand above his head. "Who knows? You're just out there, man. And it might be great or it might be total free fall, you know?"

"I know." I leaned back against one of the record bins. Free fall. My throat tightened.

"Well, listen at me go on. What's your major, anyway?"

"Me? Oh, um. Art."

"You look like an art major. Where you in school at?"

"Uh, over at . . . uh, Pratt Institute."

"Now that's a good school. You really gonna drop out?"

"I, uh—I sorta just did."

"Holy shit!" Gram guffawed, slapping his hand down on the counter. "You don't waste no time!"

"No, I guess I don't."

"Hey, you didn't forget about our party, did you? We're having one Thursday after next. You think you can make it?"

"I have to, um, I have to see if I can get off work." Why was I lying to him so much? Once I'd started, it was hard to stop.

"I hear that. You just tell the boss to give you the night off, because we are going to have a serious G. T."

"A G. T.?"

"A *good time*." He grinned. I thought about Travis and how he didn't like Gram. I wondered how I'd sneak out. It wasn't like at home, where I could just drop out of the window. And once I was out, how was I supposed to get back in?

"I guess I oughta let you look around." Gram sat back. "Anything I can help you find today?"

"Nothing in particular." I had a little money, but I hadn't planned on shopping. "I just thought I'd come in and say hi."

"Really? I'm flattered. Hi, then." Gram leaned forward on the counter again, smiling his bright smile.

"Hi."

* * *

When I got back to the apartment, Travis was packing up his guitars for rehearsal.

"How was your day, dear?" Our old routine.

"Ehhh," I growled. "Actually, it was pretty good."

"Oh yeah?" He looked up. "Square pizza in the cafeteria? Or is it all red wine and veal piccata over there?"

"What's veal piccata?" I dumped my backpack on the floor. Travis laughed. "Just a fancy way to eat a cow, that's all." He picked up his guitar cases. "Tell your mom I'll be home late."

"Sure," I said, helping him with the door. He always told me to tell her that. But he always came home before she did, anyway.

I was surprised at how easy it was to be a dropout. I'd get on the subway in the morning, same as always, and ride into the city. But I'd get off downtown, usually at Astor Place or Bleecker Street, somewhere near Mom's old neighborhood. I'd get break-fast and then, when it opened, I'd go into Barnes & Noble, up to the second floor, where I could sit with a cup of coffee and the *Village Voice* and watch the people on the street below. Read-ing the *Voice* made me think about money. About all the things I wanted to do and the money I didn't have to do them with. But I wasn't some schoolkid anymore, and I had plenty of time now to take care of the money problem. I felt older already, sit-ting in my perch, reading the *Voice*. I read the sex column and the horoscope and thought about what kinds of jobs I could get. I thought about being a waitress in a music club. Or a bar-tender. How old did you have to be to go to bartending school?

After a while, I'd leave the bookstore and explore the city. I walked around NYU, thinking I'd run into Gram. Washington

Square Park became my favorite place to hang out and read. There was a boy who came there every day with his acoustic guitar to play Bob Dylan songs. After each one, he'd thank the people who stood around listening. "Thank you. Thank you very much. That was 'Positively Fourth Street' by Bob Dylan." I saved change to throw in his guitar case. I thought a lot about what Gram said. About free fall. But I didn't feel scared anymore. I was still glad to be in New York. It felt like anything could happen here. It felt like something *was* happening. I mean, there I was, doing nothing, just sitting in a park, and I was being entertained. In New York, there was somebody willing to play you Bob Dylan's entire back catalog if you cared to stop and listen, and that was just in one tiny part of the city. Back home, you could drive all over town, but pretty much the only thing to do if you skipped school was go home and watch *The Price Is Right.*

I didn't drift like that for too long. I'd been skipping school for about a week when I came downstairs to find a big black car parked in front of the strip club. The window whirred down as I went past.

"Maria." I turned. It was Nina. "Get in the car."

"I'm—I'm on my way to school," I lied.

"No you're not. You haven't been at school all week. Get in, please. I'm late."

I was too surprised to argue. I obeyed, stumbling a little as I slid in next to Nina on the warm leather back seat.

"Did my mom find out?" I asked.

"Victoria barely knows what day of the week it is." Nina took off her gloves. The driver swerved into the empty street and accelerated onto the BQE. "The school called your grandmother, and she called me." Nina pulled a cell phone out of her purse and flipped it open. She punched the numbers.

"Here." She handed the phone to me. "Tell her you haven't been abducted by a street gang, please."

I pressed the phone to my ear. My stomach dropped. I was sure I was about to be the first casualty of a phone call. Death by Condescending Tone.

"Hello?" Grandmother was wide awake, even at seven a.m.

"Hi, Grandmother?" My voice nearly broke. "It's Maria."

"Maria, thank God. Where have you been? What's going on up there?"

"Everything's fine. I—"

"It certainly isn't fine," she bellowed. "Do you have any idea the strings I had to pull to get you into that school? The money I've spent?"

"I'll get a job. I'll pay you back—"

"I don't want you to pay me back. I want an end to this nonsense. First this melodrama with your father, now you disappear from school and your mother's phone is disconnected."

"We moved. I told Dad—" I gripped the car door as we flew down the highway.

"For heaven's sake, Maria, you know you have to tell your father something at least fifty times before he remembers. Why wasn't I privy to this information?"

"I—I don't know. I just didn't think—"

"No, you certainly didn't *think*. And I wish for the life of me you'd explain why a smart girl like yourself continues to act without thinking."

I didn't answer. Rhetorical question, anyway. I felt my

cheeks burning hot. Out the window, I watched as Nina's driver took the exit for the Brooklyn Bridge. As soon as we got off the BQE, we came to a quick stop at the back of a packed lane of traffic.

"I'm sorry, Grandmother."

"You should be! You've got your father and me both worried sick. And, as far as that school goes, you're done with it. I've been duped into this situation once, and I won't be duped into it again."

"But I—" I suddenly realized what she was talking about. She figured that I was just like my mom, taking her money and running off to the city and then dropping out of Pratt.

"I've spoken to Mrs. Dowd," Grandmother said. It took me a second to remember that Mrs. Dowd was Nina. "She's going to arrange for you to be picked up in the mornings and dropped off in the afternoons. You'll attend the public school, and if you don't like it, tough. Your other option is to come home, re-enroll at Langley, and I will pay the tuition. But I'm not funding any more shenanigans. You hear?"

I looked over at Nina, touching up her lipstick in a compact mirror. She caught my eye and raised her eyebrows.

"Yes, ma'am."

"I hate to think about what goes on in those public schools up there, but this is what happens when we don't do what's expected of us, isn't it?"

"Yes, ma'am."

"And I do hope you'll call your father. Maybe you can explain to him what's going on, because I certainly don't understand it."

"Yes, ma'am."

"You behave yourself, now. I love you, Maria."

"I love you, too, Grandmother."

She hung up the phone. I handed the cell back to Nina, trying not to cry in front of her. We were inching along the Brooklyn Bridge, stuck behind an accident.

"Your grandmother thinks she's called your bluff." Nina snapped her mirror closed. "She thinks that one day in a Brooklyn public school is going to send you running back to the familiar arms of your old prep school."

"So what" was all I could think to say.

"So, I think she's right. The school you would have to attend is, unfortunately, notorious for its violence. You won't be happy—"

"I wasn't happy at Prince."

"Don't interrupt me while I'm offering you an out."

I shut my mouth. Nina didn't sound as angry as my grandmother, but she meant business.

"Maria, what do you want to do?" She turned and looked at me, her mouth a curt line.

"Do about what?"

"I mean, what do you want to do with the rest of your life? What do you want to be when you grow up?"

I laughed. I didn't know why. At Langley and at Prince, in the short time I'd been there, they were always trying to get us to think about college, even as far back as eighth grade. In the last year, everyone became obsessed with their SAT scores. I didn't care, though. The only reason I went to Langley was because my grandmother thought private school was the only way to get a proper education. But I didn't care about proper. I was just trying to make it out in one piece.

"I don't really want to go to college." It was the first time I'd said it out loud. I expected Nina to get upset and try to convince me otherwise, but she didn't.

"What are your interests? Are you an artist, like your mother?"

"No. I like art, but I'm really bad at it." I hadn't inherited my mother's talent. My art class forays were all lame still-life sketches and crookedly thrown pots that ended up holding my dad's pencil stubs and tire pressure gauges out in the garage.

"So, what else? What do you like? What are you good at?"

"I dunno. In school, I'm good in French and English. History. But I like . . . I like music."

"Do you play an instrument?"

"No." I thought about Travis showing me the chords on his guitar when I first got to New York. I hadn't touched a musical instrument since then. "Not really. I just like listening to music. I like reading about the bands and, I was thinking, if there was some job where I could just—" I stopped, realizing how silly it sounded.

"Where you could just what?"

"Where I could just listen to music all day long. Like, maybe work in a record store or something. I dunno."

"That makes sense, considering your parents. I never did understand why your father would come to New York City to be a country singer. You'd think Nashville would've been more appropriate."

"He came to— *My* father? To be a country singer?"

"I thought you knew this." Nina rolled her eyes. "He wanted to be the next Kris Kristofferson, or somebody."

"I thought he— He told me he came to New York to work for his uncle Vin's trucking company." When my grandfather first emigrated from Italy, he came to New York. He ended up in Atlanta because of the company he worked for, and he met my grandmother and stayed. Supposedly we still had family all over New York and New Jersey, but my grandmother lost touch with them when my grandfather died.

"He may well have. But as far as I know, he was a bouncer in a dance club. Which is, I believe, where your mother met him. He was trying to be a folksinger or something on the side. I thought this was a well-known story."

"Not to me." The car lurched ahead. We'd finally passed the accident, and now we were driving at top speed over the bridge, rushing toward Manhattan.

"Back to the topic at hand. What I'm offering you is this: education. It's ridiculous to think that, here you are, in a city full of the finest art, music, and architecture in the world, and instead of experiencing it, you'll be sitting in some stuffy, over-crowded classroom somewhere in the bowels of Brooklyn, waiting for your turn at the chalkboard to solve for x." Nina raised an eyebrow at me. "I didn't care much for school myself."

"So, what do you want me to do? Go to some other school?"

"No. You'll come to my apartment. Every morning, nine o'clock sharp. I'll teach you everything you really need to know."

"Will it—will it count?"

"We'll make it count."

"What about Grandmother?"

"I'll handle her." Nina smiled. "I think she'd rather I kept my eye on you, anyway."

I looked out the window, watching City Hall blur past. Public school, or hanging out with Nina and talking about architecture all day. Did I really need to think about it?

"So when do we start?"

Nina got out of the car at a huge bank in Midtown, then had her driver take me back home. When I got there, Mom was awake, drinking coffee at the kitchen table.

"You're home early," she said.

"Teacher in-service. You're up early."

"Your grandmother called." Mom drained her cup. "You really thought Lady Hawkeye wouldn't catch you cutting classes from eight hundred miles away? She sees *all*, kiddo."

"I guess I was pretty dumb." I sat down at the kitchen table.

"Ah, she'll get over it." She got up for a refill. "You want some coffee?"

"Sure."

"So you're stuck in public school now. How do you take it?"

"It's no big deal. It's my own fault, anyway."

"No, how do you take your coffee?"

"Oh. A little milk and a lot of sugar." Mom went to the fridge. "Actually, um . . . Nina offered to homeschool me."

My mother laughed, a deep snort that sounded like tearing paper.

"Nina? Nina *Dowd*? Wants to homeschool you?" She closed the fridge door. "I know I haven't been up very long, but that's the craziest thing I've heard all day."

"She says she'll take me to museums and the opera and stuff. She says she'll teach me her business."

"You don't need to know her business." Mom put the coffee

cup in front of me. "I know she may seem smart and like she's got her shit together and all, but trust me—she'll turn on you."

"Yeah, well." I guess she was thinking about losing the apartment on Rivington. "I don't see what it could hurt. She just wants me to experience the city."

"It could hurt *you*, kiddo. Nina looks out for Nina. And her business—her husband was a creep. All the people she deals with are creeps." She sat down, rubbing her eyes. "Just don't get involved with her, okay? Just go to the regular school like a regular person. Will you trust me on this, please?"

"I trust you," I told her. But I didn't see what was so bad about Nina. In fact, the more I thought about it, the more I figured, just because my mom was upset about the apartment, why should I have to suffer? After all, Nina didn't totally kick her out. She offered us this new place in Brooklyn, and it was fine.

"At least you don't have to wear a uniform in public school," she said. Then she sat up suddenly, as if the caffeine had kicked in all at once. "Oh my gosh! You totally need new clothes! For a new start!" She grabbed my hand. "Shopping spree!"

Mom forgot all about Nina and started plotting our shopping trip. I smiled and sipped my coffee.

7

Trash and Vaudeville was crammed full of clothes that were way too cool for me. Like thigh-high patent-leather boots and metal-studded belts and torn-up T-shirts with pictures of Sid Vicious. Mom and Travis had talked me into trying on a pair of slinky black pants that were so tight, I had trouble breathing. With my skinny legs, I looked like a pair of scissors.

"Those are killer," Mom decided.

"Yeah, they're killing *me*." I unbuttoned the top and exhaled. Then I caught a glimpse of the price tag, and I almost couldn't breathe again. "Why don't we shop at Nina's boutique? Doesn't she give you an employee discount?"

"We're not shopping at Nina's." Mom sighed, irritated. "Rich old lady clothes. Anyway, quit looking at the price tags. It's on me."

We'd been all over downtown already. Mom had bought me a bunch of vintage blouses and pre-ripped punk rock T-shirts and a pair of saddle shoes, charging it all to her credit card. It was fun at first, but now I was tired and ready to get back into my comfortable old baggy jeans and sweatshirt. And I knew it had to be costing my mom a small fortune.

"Try this on with those pants." Mom thrust a silk button-down shirt at me. It was bloodred, with silver buttons and silver thread. "This shirt is so hot. It's totally Mick Jagger."

I went into the dressing room. The shirt was as tight as the pants, and the buttons only went about halfway up my chest. When I came out to look at myself in the full-length mirror, Travis was trying on a leather jacket.

"Where's Mom?"

"She went out to smoke." He looked at me. "Wow."

"I know." I tugged at the red silk, trying to cover my chest. "It's way too tight, isn't it?"

"No, it's, uh—it looks really good." But he was blushing and looking down at the jacket he had on, suddenly very interested in the zippers on the sleeves. Before I knew it, I was blushing, too. I felt like I might as well have come out of the dressing room in my underwear.

"Okay, I was totally right about that outfit." Mom came back in, swishing down the tight aisle. "You are so hot in that!"

"I can't wear this to school," I muttered.

"So . . . what if you get asked out on a date?" She gave me a mischievous look. "You can't wear a black sweatshirt every day of your life. Right, Travis?" She turned to him. He was taking off the leather jacket. "We've got the male perspective right here. What do you think, honey?" Mom threw her arm around my shoulder. "She's totally hot, right? Total boy magnet?"

"Yeah." Travis hung up the jacket, barely looking. "Very magnetic."

"See? There you go." Mom pulled at the shirt, adjusting the collar. "Amazing. You have such a perfect body, it's sick. You *have* to model. When Lee gets back from Milan, we're totally setting up headshots for you. He works with models all the time—he is so going to freak out when he sees you."

"Can I take this off now?"

"Sure, but I don't see why you'd want to."

Mom sat at the kitchen table, clipping pictures of rock stars out of old copies of *Rolling Stone* and *Spin* to decorate the new refrigerator. It was Sunday night; Travis was gone to rehearsal and I was trying to put together an outfit to wear the next morning.

"Hey, Mom?"

"Hey, kid."

"Was my dad . . . did he move to New York to become a country singer?"

"Yeah, he did, actually." She laughed, shaking her head. "Your dad and his misbegotten country career. I'd forgotten all about that. Why do you ask?"

"No reason." I turned my attention back to the clothes. "Just wondering."

"Why don't you wear that pink skirt tomorrow? With the green blouse?" Mom called out over the stereo. She had another Patti Smith record on. The third one, *Easter*. She told me it was the comeback record, after Patti broke her neck when she fell off a stage opening for Bob Seger.

"I think if I had to open for Bob Seger, I'd wanna break my neck, too," Mom joked when she put on the record. I didn't say anything. My dad loved Bob Seger.

"I was thinking for the first day I could wear something less . . ." Outrageous? I wasn't all that crazy about the hot-pink kilt skirt Mom had insisted on buying. Or the lime-green blouse that went with it. But she insisted.

"You want to make a good first impression," Mom reminded me.

"But I don't wanna . . . stand out too much. It's bad enough I'm almost six feet tall."

"You so have to get over this hang-up about your height." She sighed and put her magazine down. "When you meet Lee, he'll tell you. Short for models is five foot eight." She came over to the futon to take a look at the clothes.

"What about this?" She matched the skirt with a thin black sweater silk-screened with a picture of Edie Sedgwick. "More low key than lime green?"

"Better."

She held the green blouse up to me. "You may have been right about this blouse. It's not your best color."

"It would look good on you."

"Really?" She held it up to her own face. "It doesn't wash me out?"

"No. Why don't you take it?"

"Seriously?"

"You're the one who bought it in the first place."

"Cool!" She held the sleeves out. "I'm probably too short for it, though."

"I'll fix it for you."

"You are the awesomest." She kissed my cheek and took the blouse back to her bedroom to try it on.

"I was thinking I could come with you tomorrow, if you

want. To help you register, or whatever," she called from behind the cracked door.

"Um, that's okay," I called back. "I can handle it."

"I should've known what was going on, shouldn't I?" She walked back into the hallway in the green blouse, the sleeves dangling. "I mean, you could've talked to me. If you were so unhappy in that school."

"It's not your fault." I sat down on the futon. "I'm not used to . . . I dunno. I just usually deal with this stuff on my own."

"I'm not doing too great with the whole mom thing, am I?" She pushed her sleeves up, frowning. "I know I'm not. But I want you to feel like you can talk to me. Like we can be friends, at least. I just—I need you to help me figure this out."

"Figure what out?"

"This whole . . . this whole being your mother! I feel like I'm really shitty at it." She scowled. "See, right there? I shouldn't have said 'shitty.' That's not very motherly."

"It's nothing I haven't heard before. Anyway, look. It's not like you left me in the car with the windows rolled up. I shouldn't have cut school. But we were moving, and you were working—you don't have to look over my shoulder all the time. I'm old enough now; I can take care of myself."

"I know." She sat down next to me on the futon. "You grew up so fast. I kept meaning to— I mean, it feels like I left for the weekend when you were a little kid, and now you're all grown-up. All of a sudden. And I'm not sure how it happened." Her voice broke a little. "The time just got away from me somehow."

"Don't worry about it." I put my hand on her shoulder. "We're catching up now."

"I'm glad we are." She stood up, and a switch flipped. She went from sounding like she was about to cry to smiling her wide smile again. "It is *so* much fun buying clothes for you. Do you have any idea, if I had your body, how much debt I'd be in right now?" Before I could tell her that I'd rather have *her* body, she was back on the topic of school.

"Now, are you sure, are you totally positive, that you don't want me to come with you tomorrow?"

"I'm sure. It's just school. I can deal."

"Because I don't offer to get up before nine a.m. for just anyone, you know?"

"I'm positive. I'll be fine."

"In that case, I'm going to go put on something that fits, and then let's go to the diner. I'm so in the mood for pancakes. How 'bout you?"

"I could go for pancakes."

"Excellent!" Mom ran back to her bedroom, and I sank into the futon, relieved. If she'd insisted on going with me to the public school tomorrow, I don't know how I would have explained the driver in the big black car on the corner, waiting to take me to Nina's place uptown.

Nina's apartment was huge. I couldn't get over it. The kitchen was almost as big as our entire apartment in Brooklyn. The living room was completely white—white carpet, white sofa, white drapes—and wrapped with windows that looked out over Central Park and the eruption of skyscrapers in Midtown. I couldn't stop gawking at everything. The white marble sculpture on its own pedestal in the foyer. The chrome-and-glass coffee table with the black-and-white photography books and copies of the *New Yorker*. The painting on the white wall of a single red circle, a thick, cautionless brushstroke on a plain white canvas. This place was even nicer than my grandmother's.

"You have a beautiful apartment, Mrs. Dowd."

"Thank you, and call me Nina." She stood in the hallway, buttoning her coat. "I thought we'd start with the Hopper exhibit at the Whitney. And then, this afternoon, there's a Godard retrospective starting at Film Forum. Are you sure you won't be cold in that skirt?"

"I'm fine." I tugged at the pink kilt. It was shorter than I remembered it being when I tried it on.

"Good. Then let's go. You've had breakfast, I trust?"

"Yes, ma'am."

"My God." She stopped, her hand on the doorknob. "You Southerners are charming, aren't you?" She jerked her chin. "Our chariot awaits."

She whisked out the door. In her heels, Nina was as tall as I was, but I had to double-time to keep up.

I couldn't concentrate on the book Nina had given me to read. I kept getting distracted, watching the traffic grind along the BQE and wondering how mad my mom was going to be when she found out I was lying to her.

"Hey, Loudmouth." Travis pulled the headphones off my ears.

"Ow!" I swatted him. "What gives?"

"Nothin'. Just checking up on you." He sat down on the edge of the futon, loosening his bootlaces. "You barely said two words all afternoon."

"I'm fine."

"Yeah? You sure about that?"

"I'm just trying to read." I put my headphones back on, but Travis kept talking.

"That's a pretty thick book. The new school's hard?"

"Mm-hmm." I tried to look extra studious.

"Well, listen, you wanna take a break? Come hear the band?"

"What?" I took off my headphones.

"We finally got a singer. She's really great. And she's a chick." Travis pulled his bootlaces tight. "I think you'd really like her. You know, with all your superchick music and everything."

"My superchick music?" I laughed.

"Whatever it's called. Your tapes." Travis latched his guitar case. "You don't have to come. I just thought you'd be into it. And I figured this new school's probably a drag, and you might wanna get your mind off it. Anyway . . ." He cleared his throat. "We'll probably get a gig soon and you can come hear us then, so, it's no big deal. If you're busy."

I thought about it. Travis didn't usually invite me to tag along with him. And I wanted to hear his band. There was no telling when Mom would be home. So, why not?

"I guess the reading can wait." I got up and grabbed my coat.

From the outside, the rehearsal studio looked like the kind of abandoned warehouse where a movie villain would be training a team of ninjas. I followed Travis inside, past a smoky lounge and through a heavy door that led to a smoky hallway. Muffled music thumped out of each door—ska-punk, metal, disco covers. At the end of the hallway, Travis's band was waiting outside one of the rehearsal rooms. I recognized Slade from moving day.

"Hey, man," Travis said. "What gives?"

"The hippies are still at it," Slade said. "Sherry went to go tell Larry. They're totally eating our rehearsal time again." Slade banged his fist against the door. "Time's up, hippies!" he shouted, to no avail. Their gurgling music droned on behind the door.

"So, Trav, you kicked the old lady to the curb?" A heavyset guy in dark glasses and a Motorhead T-shirt gave Travis a grin.

"Nah, this is my old lady's kid. Maria, this is our drummer, Gary."

"Hi." I reached out my hand to shake his, but Gary just nodded. I stuck my hand back in my pocket and tried to pretend I was still cool.

"You guys care if she hangs out while we rehearse?" Travis asked. "Today was her first day at this shitty school, so I thought, you know."

"It's all good," Gary said. I cleared my throat and looked down at my shoes. Somehow, I felt even worse lying to Travis about school than I did to my mom.

"I've got reinforcements!" A girl with bright pink hair called out from down the hallway. Behind her was a short, stern-faced guy with his hair in long dreadlocks and his beard shaved into a pointy triangle. He wore a T-shirt that said SLAYER and leather boots that went up to his knees.

"All right." He opened the rehearsal room door and barged right through, no nonsense. "China Cat Sunflowers, time to wrap it up. Your fellow renters need the time they paid for." He marched back out, shaking his head. "Freakin' Dead cover bands, man." He looked at me. "What're you gonna do?"

"Thanks, Larry," the girl with the pink hair said. "Larry runs the place." She leaned over to me. "He's the bomb."

We waited in the hallway while the hippies packed up their gear. Travis introduced me to the pink-haired girl.

"Sherry, this is Maria. My girlfriend's kid."

"Hey." The girl shook my hand. "I'm totally changing my name, by the way. Right now I'm deciding between Holly Terror and Penny Dreadful. Which one do you like better?"

"As a name? Um . . ." The last of the hippies shoved past us, and I followed Travis and the guys into the rehearsal room. It stank of bitter pot smoke.

"Fuckin' reeks in here!" Gary coughed. "Fuckin' hippies and their fuckin' pot! It's like fuckin' skunks and feet!"

"Hey, Gary. Chill, man." Travis unlatched his guitar case.

"We gotta get another rehearsal space," Gary muttered, unpacking his snare drum.

"So, what do you think?" Sherry slung her silver-glittered guitar over her shoulder. "About the whole name thing."

"I like 'Penny Dreadful.'" I sat down on the sunken purple couch in the corner. The dirty gray carpet was littered with coiled pieces of guitar strings and broken picks.

"That's the one I like, too!" She brightened. "And it means something, too. They used to have these, like, pulp comic books over in England, and they only cost a penny. Get it, Penny Dreadful?"

"Check it out—hippie leftovers." Slade held up an acoustic guitar. "Dumb stoners left a Martin behind the bass amp." He handed it to Travis.

"Damn." Travis brushed his thumb along the strings. "This is a nice guitar."

"Sounds like they were too stoned to tune it," Slade said. Travis strummed it again, tuning the lowest string.

"Kum-baa-yaa," Sherry/Penny sang, laughing. "Isn't acoustic music, like, the most boring thing on the planet? I swear, if one more band goes 'unplugged,' I think I'm gonna puke."

I started to say that I thought it was pretty cool when Nirvana did it, but I didn't want to embarrass Travis. I watched him, his head bent over the guitar, the back of his neck pale white.

"It's just an alternate tuning," he murmured. "Like Joni Mitchell." Travis pressed his fingers to the guitar and made an odd-sounding chord.

"Joni fuckin' Mitchell?" Gary whacked his snare, laughing. "Hey, man, we—"

"Don't say her name like that," Travis snapped at Gary. "Joni Mitchell's a genius." Travis bent back over the guitar. Gary gave a nervous chuckle.

"Sorr-*ree*." Gary held up his hands. "I didn't know you were down with the hippie music."

"I don't give a shit about hippie music. But Joni Mitchell's different." Travis plucked the strings, a gentle, rolling pattern. "And you don't have to say her name like that. With a fuckin' profanity in it. Okay?" He looked up at Gary, his eyes steely.

"Okay, dude." Gary gave Slade a look, and Slade shrugged, tuning his bass.

"Hey, guys," Penny jumped in. "I brought those new songs from last week. I worked out the lyrics. Which one do you want to do first, 'Society Kills' or 'Police Brutality'?"

"What was the one with the really fast chorus?" Slade plugged his bass into the amp. "Remember?" He thunked out a rapid succession of notes. Gary joined in with a speeding drum roll that seemed to accelerate like a car engine. Travis finally looked up from the guitar.

"It sounded nice," I told him. "What you were playing."

"What?" he shouted over the drums.

I shook my head and mouthed, "Forget it." He put the hippie guitar back behind the bass amp and picked up his electric. He plugged in and joined Slade and Gary's riot. Penny plugged her guitar in, too, and stepped up to the microphone to shout above the music as she thrashed out the chords.

> *I can't be what they want me to be!*
> *Society kills! Society kills!*
> *Get married, get a job, and be happy!*
> *Society kills! Society kills!*

I sat back on the sofa and felt the music vibrating in my bones. I remembered the earplugs Travis had given me, and I squished them into my ears. The drums dulled to a low roar, and I could hear Travis's guitar, sharper now, rising above Slade's pulsing bass and the crunch of Penny's distorted chords. Travis's sound seemed to soar out of him, each note lifting off his fingers and flying like a spark. I couldn't stop watching him, watching his fingers flutter along the neck of the guitar, then stop, the sustained wails hanging there for a moment, then disappearing as he attacked again, bending the strings, streaking the notes across the song like meteors flashing in a dark sky. He looked up, and I caught his eye. Immediately I wanted to look away, but I couldn't. I felt like I'd caught him in the middle of something, like I'd seen him naked, seen him as something else. In that moment, with his guitar, he stopped being Travis, Mom's boyfriend. He started being someone else entirely.

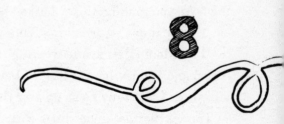

8

Going to Gram's party that Thursday night was easier than I thought it would be. No sneaking around required. Well, no sneaking. But more lies.

"I knew you'd be a hit!" Mom was so excited when I told her I'd been invited to a party. "Maybe public school won't be so bad after all."

"Maybe not," I agreed.

So far, studying with Nina was the most fun I'd had in school since second grade with Miss Miller and her room full of terrariums. Nina would take me to museums in the mornings, then to the library to check out books on the artists we'd seen. Then we went back to her apartment, where she let me type essays on her computer while she made phone calls and went to meetings. She'd come back and print out the essays to mail off to my grandmother; then we'd eat a late lunch and go to a matinee of some documentary or something foreign with subtitles. Nina's driver would wind through the streets of the

Upper East Side, Nina pointing out the various styles of the buildings as we passed, and the histories, the families who lived there. She seemed to know everything about everything—who built the buildings, who painted the paintings, what period they belonged to, their lost loves, and why they died in anguish.

"Are you grading this?" I asked her.

"Yes, but don't worry. I'm giving you As."

I let Mom talk me into wearing the tight black pants from Trash and Vaudeville, but I didn't have the courage for the red silk shirt. I laced my boots up over the pant legs and wore one of Travis's thermal undershirts with a ripped T-shirt over it.

"That's more like it," Travis said when he saw the outfit. We were leaving the apartment at the same time—he was headed out to meet up with Slade and Gary for poker night.

"You think it's okay? This outfit?" Mom was working late, so she didn't see which clothes I finally decided on.

"It's way better than that baggy-ass shit you usually wear."

"Hey, don't knock my baggy-ass shit. It's comfortable."

"It's enough clothes for a family of four. Which way are you going?" We jogged down the subway steps side by side.

"Manhattan. Where's your bike?"

"It's on the fritz. I got a buddy coming to look at it this weekend." He dropped a token into the slot. "So who from P.S. whatever lives in Manhattan?" I followed behind him at the turnstile. I don't know why, but I felt like telling him the truth.

"Can you keep a secret?"

"Depends." He shrugged.

"I haven't been going to the public school. Nina set it up. She's homeschooling me. I've been going uptown to her apartment every day this week."

Travis just looked at me. A line of worry jagged its way across his brow.

"So whose party is this? Nina's?"

"Remember that guy from the record store? Gram?"

"You're kidding me." He rubbed his forehead. "The fat kid?"

"Yeah."

"Man." He kicked at the graffitied bench on the subway platform. "I don't know who to worry about more, you or your mother."

"You don't have to worry about either of us. It's just a party."

"Yeah, but . . ." He scratched the back of his neck. "Look, I don't totally get this thing between your grandmother and your mom—"

The train came roaring into the station. We got on. The doors slid closed and the train careened off down the tracks. Travis and I sat down. He picked up where he'd left off.

"I was saying, I don't get it, okay? But what I do know is, if you piss off your grandma and she stops sending those checks up here, it won't be too good for any of us."

"What checks?"

"The ones your grandma sends to Vic every month to take care of you. How do you think she could afford all those clothes she bought you? We barely scrape by."

The train screeched around a curve, and I planted my feet to steady myself.

"I didn't realize I was such a cash cow," I said.

"I didn't mean it like that."

"You think that's the reason why—" I didn't want to say it. "Is that why she agreed to let me move in with you guys? So she could get the money?"

"Maria, come on. The money's for you. Besides, you're her kid. She's your mom. She loves you."

"I know." The train slowed, coming to a stop at the next station. The doors slid open, but no one got on. "I know she does."

Gram's directions were perfect. I found the building, the elevator, then "straight on down the hallway till you smell the chicken frying." The suite was crowded and hot. I took off my jacket and was looking for a place to stow it when two guys carrying brown paper sacks, one dressed in a Dallas Cowboys jersey, the other in a sport coat, came in and announced themselves to the crowd.

"People! Do not fear! The Texans are here!" A loud cheer went up, and I escaped to the kitchen to look for Gram. Instead, I found a potluck supper spread out all over the table and countertops—macaroni and cheese, fried okra, sweet potatoes, green bean casserole, bowls of chips and Ro-Tel dip, plates full of fried chicken, and four plastic pitchers of tea, one of them marked UNSWEET in sturdy black letters.

"Stand back, hot biscuits here!" A short, bearded guy in a flannel shirt yanked a cookie sheet out of the oven, using his shirttail as a hot mitt. He dropped the biscuits onto the stove top with a clatter, then jumped to the sink to run his hand under the cold water.

"Damn!" He noticed me. "Oh, hey. Did you just come in with Seth and Jesse?"

"No, uh, I was looking for Gram, actually?" My voice went up, making it sound like I was asking a question. "He invited me."

"You must be Maria. He told me about you. I'm Sandy."
He wiped his hand on his pant leg and held it out to me. "One
of Gram's roommates."

"The philosophy major?"

"Physics." He smiled. "You were close."

"Hey, Sandy," the Texan in the sport coat interrupted, holding up two six-packs of Pabst Blue Ribbon. "The cooler's full.
You got any more room in the fridge?"

"I don't know, man. I think we better start drinking faster."
Sandy chuckled.

"You want one?" The Texan held one of the six-packs out
to me.

"Sure, thanks." I took the entire six-pack out of his hands.
He and Sandy both howled.

"Now, that's my kind of woman!" the Texan exclaimed.

"Look out, now, Gram's got dibs." Sandy took another pitcher
of tea out of the fridge and squeezed the six-pack in, breaking
off one for himself and one for the Texan, who went back to re-
join the party. I handed him the six-pack I'd taken as a joke.

"Seriously, you want one?" Sandy loosened another can
from the plastic rings.

"No, thanks. I'd rather have a glass of tea."

"Man, tell me about it." Sandy closed the refrigerator door.
"These people up here just do not understand. Putting a pack
of sugar in an unsweet tea just ain't the same." He opened the
freezer and scooped a couple of ice cubes into a jelly glass with
a picture of Dale Earnhardt on it, then filled it with tea.

"All the big glasses are gone, but we have a free-refill policy."

"Thanks." I took the glass and drank.

"Come on, I'll take you back to Gram's room."

I followed Sandy down the hallway, to one of the closed doors.

"Hey, Gram? Maria's here." Sandy knocked, then opened the door. Gram sat straddled against the back of his desk chair, his sleeve rolled up. Another boy was bent studiously over his arm as two others looked on.

"What in the sam hell are y'all doing?" Sandy asked.

"Gettin' tattoos. You want one?"

"Hell, yeah." Sandy leaned in to inspect more closely. "What're you gettin'?"

"Our logo. Hey, Maria. You want a tattoo?"

"No, thanks." I had to look away before I got queasy. I stared up at the wall opposite Gram's bed, at two posters hanging side by side. One was a black-and-white shot of Henry Rollins shouting into a microphone. The other was a full-color shot of a young Dolly Parton.

"Needles make me kind of nauseous," I explained.

"Oh, hey, you don't have to hang out in here, then. I'll be done in just a second."

"Okay. I'll just be—I'll be outside, then." I backed out of the room and went to the living room to find a corner to hide in. I gravitated toward the stereo, where the Texan in the Cowboys jersey was arguing with a black girl who was nearly as tall as I was.

"Man, Natalie, come on," he said. "Take off this Björk shit. I made us a mixtape. Special, just for tonight."

"Seth, I happen to like this Björk shit." She rolled her eyes at him.

"It's not as good as the Sugarcubes. Lookit, I promise, you're so gonna love this mixtape. It's got Matthew Sweet *and* Merle Haggard."

"Fine, be my guest." Natalie hit a button and the Björk CD popped out of the stereo. Seth put his tape in and pressed play. Country music came out of the speakers. Natalie saw me and smiled.

"It's like this every time. First they want to hear all the old country music and reminisce about how they used to watch *Hee Haw* with their granddads. Then they start talking about how they're so glad they got out of the South, away from all those fucking rednecks and their dumbass country music." She shook her head. "Then from, like, two a.m. till dawn, it's nothing but Wu Tang and Bone Thugs-n-Harmony. You must be Maria."

"Word travels fast." I was surprised.

"Gram told me about you. He said he'd finally met a girl taller than me."

"Yeah, I guess I'm, uh, tall." I laughed, feeling a weird buzz in my head that wasn't coming from the iced tea. Had Gram told everyone at the party about me?

"I'm Natalie, by the way. I hope you don't think it's weird. That we're friends."

"Huh?"

"Gram and I. I mean, we dated so long ago. Last year."

"Oh."

"He's a really great guy." She put her hand on my arm. "I mean, that's why we're still friends. He really knows how to treat a woman."

"Oh," I repeated. I didn't know what else to say. I couldn't believe Gram had talked so much about me. And to his ex-girlfriend. For a moment I felt in over my head, and I wanted to get outside somehow, take a breath of fresh air. I wondered if Travis was right about Gram. I wished Travis was there—and I was surprised at myself for wishing it.

"So, you're at Pratt?"

"Me?" It took a second to realize that Natalie was still talking to me. "Oh, uh, sort of. I just dropped out."

"Really? I thought Pratt was supposed to be so great."

"Oh, it is. It's really—it's really great. Excellent school. But I needed to take a little . . . time out, you know?"

"Totally. Sometimes I so wish I'd deferred for a year after high school. But I went to a college prep school, and the pressure was unbelievable. They wanted us to start thinking about college in eighth grade!"

"Same here!"

"And it's crazy, because then you finally get to college, and you're so totally burned-out, you're just, like, 'What's my name again?'" She stuck out her tongue and made a crazy face. "I should've done what you're doing. Taken a year off, bummed around Europe. Or just stayed at home, not thinking."

"Totally." I gulped my tea, wondering what to say next. "So, what's your major?"

"Microbiology."

"Ah." I nodded. Wow, what do you say to that? "Like biology, only smaller."

Natalie broke into a loud guffaw that caused several of the people standing around to turn and stare.

"Now I see why you and Gram get along," she remarked.

"Did I hear my name?" Enter Gram. He had his hair slicked back like a 1950s greaser.

"Gram! See what I mean?" Natalie laughed even harder. "What did you do to your hair?"

"It's my rockabilly 'do. It's Brylcreem, baby. Po-made. You like it?" He turned to give us the profile view. "And you think *that's* something, check this out." He peeled back the gauze on the inside of his forearm to show us the swollen, spidery black lines spelling out the same SSK logo that decorated his flyers.

"Gram Medley, you did not." Natalie was indignant.

"Anybody wants a tattoo, Matt's giving 'em in Sandy's room now," Gram announced. The crowd didn't seem too enthusiastic. Gram elbowed Natalie.

"I trust you've been telling Maria all kinds of wonderful things about me."

"Of course," Natalie deadpanned. "I'm not only your fan club president, I'm also a client."

"Ha, ha. Say, how's everybody doing on beverages? Maria, more tea?"

"No, thanks. I'm good."

"This is part of our mission as SSKs. We help new Southern transplants adjust to the sudden sweet-tea deficiency in their diets. Along with many, many other general survival tips for living in the Northeast."

"Yeah, like, beware the winter." Natalie's eyes widened. "You wanna know the key to survival? Layers. Layers, and long underwear."

"And you have to unlearn all your 'ma'ams,'" Seth the Texan chimed in. "It's the exact opposite of everything you learned growing up. Northern women throw a damn *fit* if you call them ma'am. They go freakin' ballistic 'cause they think you're implying that they're *old*."

"I know, dude—how hard is it to *not* say ma'am all the time?" Gram whistled. "I had no idea I was so well trained."

"Oh yeah, and get ready for everybody to make fun of your accent," Seth added. Gram and Natalie both groaned.

"I have to say, the general stupidity level is pretty astounding, as far as misconceptions about us Southerners go," Gram said. "When I got the record store job, I put on a Velvet Underground record one day, and my boss couldn't believe I'd heard of them. Not only that, he couldn't believe that you could actually *buy* a Velvet Underground record in South Carolina."

"Actually, that one kind of surprises *me*," Natalie said.

"Come on. We've got college radio. We've got TV."

"Hey, you know what really is weird?" Seth piped up again. "How come there's a Little Italy, and a Chinatown, and all those Irish neighborhoods up in the Bronx, but there's no Little South? You know, someplace we could go and drink sweet tea and eat barbecue and watch SEC basketball?"

"Well, you *could* go up to Harlem and eat barbecue, but y'all are too chickenshit for that," Natalie said, crossing her arms.

"I'm not too chickenshit for Harlem," Gram protested. "Where do you think all that okra came from?"

"Come on, you know what I meant," Seth said. "Hold on a second—you didn't fry that okra yourself?"

"Naw, man. I can't cook if it don't say 'Top Ramen' on it."

"Dang, dude." Seth shook his head. "You just shattered my world."

"The reason there's no Little South or whatever is because Southerners are too smart to move to New York City," Natalie said. "Nobody realizes how good they got it down there till they come up here. Then they go running back to their cheap rents and big trees and nice manners."

"But if it's so great down there, then why did we all move up here?" I asked. Natalie, Seth, and Gram turned and looked at me.

"That's the question we end up asking ourselves every time we have one of these parties," Seth told me.

"So, what's the answer?" I asked. They all got quiet for a second.

"Because it's *New York fucking City*," Natalie said, "and it's the coolest city in the whole wide world."

It was past midnight, and the bassy thump of the Wu-Tang Clan thrummed through the walls, just like Natalie said it would. But inside Gram's room, there was soft music playing from a portable record player on his desk.

"This is nice," I said. "Who is it?"

"You should know." He laughed. "It's your mom's record. Half that stuff y'all sold at the store I brought home for myself."

"My mom never played this." We were sitting side by side on the bed. We'd left the other SSKs to their own devices an hour ago, retreating to Gram's room to listen to his record collection and stuff ourselves silly on macaroni and cheese, biscuits, and collard greens. "She's more into Patti Smith these days."

"Can't argue with Patti Smith. Too bad she never played this one for you, though." Gram got up to retrieve the record cover. "I don't know who your mom's favorite Beatle is, but it's not this guy. It's practically brand new." The cover was a black box a quarter of an inch thick. The gray, rainy picture on the front was of a sullen-looking guy in garden boots, surrounded by a bunch of statues of gnomes. George Harrison. *All Things Must Pass.*

"I don't know if she has a favorite Beatle." I handed the album cover back to him. "She's more of a Stones fan."

"Everybody's got a favorite Beatle. Even Stones fans. I bet I can guess yours in one try."

"Bet you can't." I folded my arms.

"John Lennon."

I gave him an annoyed look. "How'd you guess?"

"Easy. Going to Pratt, you're an artist. You're probably into the whole Yoko Ono–Bagism thing."

"Bagism?"

"Yeah—*Everybody's talkin' 'bout Bagism*—you know, from 'Give Peace a Chance.' That thing where John and Yoko said everybody oughta go around dressed in bags so you wouldn't be able to see their faces, and then there wouldn't be any prejudice."

"Oh. I always thought that was just a made-up word," I confessed. "That's not a bad idea. Wearing a bag. Except how would you walk around in it?"

"That'd be the tricky part," Gram agreed. "I could've used one back in junior high, though. When I was too young to grow a beard to cover the zits."

"Now you can practice beardism," I joked.

"Only when the Braves are in the play-offs." Gram laughed. "Uh—what was I saying?"

"You were explaining how you guessed my favorite Beatle."

"Oh yeah. Well, you're a pretty serious gal, so I figured I could rule out McCartney and Ringo, since they're more on the pop side. And you never heard this"—he brandished the album cover again—"*the* greatest Beatle solo album of all time. I'm thinking you won't fully make your conversion to a George fan until we hit 'Beware of Darkness' on side three."

"Side *three*?"

"It's three separate records! Six sides altogether!" He opened the box again and showed me. "All the songs John and Paul wouldn't let him record with the band."

"So much for the Quiet Beatle," I said, and Gram laughed again.

"What makes you think I'm such a serious gal?" I asked him.

He sat back down next to me on his bed. "I can't put my finger on it, exactly. It's just something about the way you are. Maybe it's not so much serious as it is . . . sad." He reached out for my hand. "What makes you look so sad all the time?"

I bit my lip. "I dunno."

"I don't want anything to make you sad anymore." He reached out and touched my cheek. I closed my eyes. *Okay*, I thought. *This is the part where he's going to kiss me.*

"Man—'Let It Down'—is this not the greatest song ever?"

I opened my eyes. Gram's head was tilted back against the wall, his own eyes closed blissfully.

"Listen at those drums. That slide guitar. *Dang.*" He nodded his head along to the song. "I remember asking my piano teacher back at the Governor's School to teach me how to play piano like Billy Preston. And he told me pop music was just a distraction. But it's songs like this that keep me in love with music." He took his hand out of mine to play air drums along with the song.

"This is why I'm thinking about moving out to LA. Get

some sun, play in some bands. I'm never gonna hack it as some piano virtuoso. I just majored in music because my mom wanted me to go to college and it's the only thing I'm interested in. But I'd rather just play Jerry Lee Lewis, you know what I mean?"

"Sure," I said, remembering something my mom had said about Johnny Thunders. "Expertise is overrated."

"Exactly!" He slapped his thigh. "And I wonder why I'm even bothering to freeze my tail off up here when, realistically, I know I'm not the best. If you're the un-best, you just end up playing background music in some fancy restaurant for tips. Or becoming a stuffy old music teacher who holds his nose when somebody mentions Billy Preston. Man, that ain't me. I look at my heroes, and not one of 'em was a music theory genius." He pointed his thumb at Dolly Parton and Henry Rollins on the wall, and Johnny Cash on the back of the door. "I guess I'm sort of in the middle of a personality crisis at the moment. I should apologize—I don't normally go on and on like this, but I'm still not used to telling my problems to an actual person."

"Yeah, those non-actual people really know how to lend an ear."

"I know it's crazy." He blushed. "When I was little, I used to curl up under that picture of Dolly Parton every night and tell her my problems. I was just this fat little dude who played piano, so you can imagine all the friends I had in Gaffney. I used to pretend Dolly was my secret girlfriend. Then I discovered punk rock, and I started talking to Henry Rollins the way some people talk to Jesus. Then in high school I got into Johnny Cash, and following his example, I finally started talking to the real Jesus."

"Did that help?"

"Well, I met more girls at the First Baptist teen center than I did in my room with Henry, so I guess it did."

I laughed. "And what about Dolly? Should I be jealous?"

"No, no. She's still a special friend, but we've talked it over and decided we should see other people." Gram put his hand in mine again.

"That's good." My heart was beating double time. It's not as if Gram were drop-dead gorgeous, but there was something I liked about him. Something I liked a lot.

"Maria, I don't want to seem ... unseemly." He laughed nervously. "I know this is sort of like a first date. And I'm, uh, sorry—I've never been good at this."

"Good at what?" I had a twinge of fear that he was about to throw me out of his room.

"At putting the moves on someone. Especially someone like you."

"Oh." Someone like me? What did that mean? Someone tall? "Putting the moves on me—is that what this is?"

He laughed. "See? You're too cool to kiss."

"Me?" *Pfft.* Gram thought I was cool? Not even cool, but *too* cool? A college guy? I had a surge of confidence, and I did it. I leaned over and kissed him. Just like that. When I pulled away, he just sat there with his eyes closed and the same blissed-out expression on his face as when he was swept up in the George Harrison song.

"Gram," I whispered. "I am so *not* cool."

I crept into the apartment. My lips were chapped from kissing Gram through two more sides of George Harrison. I locked the door behind me, feeling light-headed. Even Citygirls was quiet.

I could hear Travis snoring softly through the closed bedroom door. As I took my jacket off, the sleeve hit the kitchen table and sent a sheet of paper curling down to the floor. I picked it up—it was a note from Mom. This time, it was a sketch of a dragon, and the words came out of its nose in puffs of smoke and flame:

Maria,
Hope you were a hit at the party! Your
grandmother called while you were out!
Call her back tomorrow—collect! She's
flying you back to Atlanta for Thanksgiving!
Strict orders! Yikes!
Gobble Gobble Hey!
Mom

9

I grabbed my seat belt for dear life as my grandmother slung her ancient Bonneville sedan around the on-ramp and hurtled into the 285 traffic.

"You look better, thank goodness," she said, whipping the wheel around to straighten the car out. "You've got color in your cheeks, and it looks like you've put on weight."

"Thanks," I said, trying to relax and breathe deeply.

"Your father should be at the house by the time we get back. And Nell's bringing over some of that Hoppin' John you like so much."

"Sounds good." Nell was another of my grandmother's neighbors, and she always brought us food at the holidays— plates of fried okra, Mason jars full of pickles and preserves, coconut cakes, homemade fudge. She had her own family gatherings, and she always made too much.

"Of course, Hoppin' John is supposed to be for New Year's

Day, not Thanksgiving," Grandmother sniffed, "but I think we can overlook it."

That was Grandmother. Sometimes it was hard to tell if she was insulting you or not.

"It sounds like things are going well with Nina Dowd. No more incidents to report?"

"No, ma'am."

"Excellent." She shot the Bonneville between two eighteen wheelers without batting an eye. I dug my feet into the floor mat, bracing for impact.

"Maria, you might find it hard to believe, but I was a teenage girl myself, once upon a time. And I had a bit of a rebellious streak. Do you think my parents wanted me marrying your grandfather? He was a traveling salesman ten years my senior, for goodness' sake. And he came here from New York City, of all godforsaken places. They couldn't decide whether to hate him more because he was an Italian immigrant or because he was a Yankee."

"I—uh—" I tried to stay upright as Grandmother merged lanes.

"I understand now, after watching your father make the mistakes he made with your mother, that we as parents must often simply sit and wait and pray that you'll get through your little adventures unscathed. And hopefully not pregnant. I don't have anything to worry about there, do I?" She took her eyes off the road to give me a steely glare.

"No, ma'am," I answered quickly. Terrific, a sex talk with my grandmother. Where's that eighteen wheeler when you need it?

"Good. Well, now we just have to get you through this year and next, get you into a good college, and that's that, isn't it?"

"Yes, ma'am. I guess—" I gasped as Grandmother floored it to pass a souped-up Honda CR-X in the slow lane. "I guess that's that."

Dad wasn't at Grandmother's yet—the holiday traffic, he told us on the answering machine. The second message was from Dory. She'd just gotten home, and they were about to go over to her mother's cousin's for dinner, but did I want to come over in the meantime?

"Don't be back too late—we eat promptly at six," Grandmother called after me as I escaped out the back. I cut across the yards and rang Dory's bell. Her mom answered. Nell Schaffer was already there, dropping off preserves.

"Come in, Maria." Mrs. Mason gave me a hug. "Happy Thanksgiving. You know Mrs. Schaffer, right?"

"Yes, ma'am." I hugged Nell. She wore a thick brown sweater embroidered with red and yellow autumn leaves.

"Oh, look at you! Isn't she so grown-up, Laura?" Nell fawned. Dory's mom, always classy with her short blond hair and impeccable outfits, agreed.

"We're very proud of her." As if I were her own kid, not just somebody who hung out with Dory.

"I was so upset when your grandmother told me you were sick." Nell shook her head mournfully. She went on before I could tell her I was fine. "When she said you were coming down for Thanksgiving, I said, Glennie, now, you let me make that girl some of my Hoppin' John, because I know she loves it, and she probably doesn't get any good home cooking up there in New York City."

"Well, I—"

"There you are!" Dory jogged down the stairs. "Come on, I have something to show you before we go." She grabbed my hand before I could say my polite good-byes.

"Thanks for the rescue," I said once we were safely behind Dory's closed bedroom door.

"Anytime. Hey, you look good. I love that sweater."

"Thanks." I tugged at my sleeves. "So, what's going on?"

"The usual." Dory rolled her eyes. "My mom and dad are already arguing over all this we-have-to-go-visit-the-family crap. I can't wait till we get there so they can start drinking."

I laughed, but I knew Dory had it good. Her parents were insanely cool. Her dad taught Eastern Religion at Emory, and her mom taught art to special-ed kids. I'd seen them have what Dory called "an argument" before. It was the nicest argument I'd ever witnessed.

"Tell me about New York," Dory said, rifling through her backpack. It was strange to be in her room now that she'd gone to college. It was like someone had taken bites out of it. Her stereo and all her best posters were gone. Her desk and bookshelves were tidy and straight. The floor, aside from the island of her spilling-over suitcase and backpack, was unnervingly clean.

"It's cool." I sat down on the bed, biting my thumbnail.

"What's your mom like?"

"She's awesome. We hang out all the time. Her boyfriend's in this really cool band. And my mom's got so many amazing records—you would totally freak out."

"Oh yeah? What kind of stuff?" She was taking everything out of her backpack now. Books, tapes, more books.

"Um, mostly New York punk stuff. Johnny Thunders. Lou Reed. Television. Patti Smith."

"I've totally been wanting to get into Patti Smith. Michael Stipe talks about her all the time in interviews. And Jeff Buckley sang on her last album."

"She's, like, so intense. You would be really into it."

"Dude, make me a mixtape."

"Okay." I'd never made Dory a mixtape before. She already had all the cool songs.

"Have you heard the new Nick Cave record? *Boatman's Call?*" she asked.

"No. Not yet."

"Ohh." Dory clutched her chest. "I'm totally in love with it. I put some songs from it on this—hang on—" She moved from the backpack to the suitcase, tossing out all the clothes.

"Duh. Here it is." She handed me a cassette decorated with a picture of Trent Reznor's head taped onto what looked like Tori Amos's body. I read the spine: *SupahGrrl Mixtape #22— Songs for the City!*

"I've been totally obsessed with Iggy Pop lately, so he's all over it, too. And there's some new Pavement stuff, and Björk—"

"Oh yeah! I heard the new Björk CD!" It was so rare that I'd actually heard a CD before one of Dory's tapes. "At this party—" I stopped, feeling like a show-off. *At this party in New York.* It sounded snobby in my head.

"It's insane, right? So good." Dory didn't seem to care about my cool party. Then I remembered that she got to go to college parties all the time. "I've also been totally obsessed with this band called Swell—have you heard this?" She held up another CD that was floating around in the sea of her suitcase. "*Too Many Days Without Thinking*? I'm starting to think this is the motto of my college years. My brain is fried. Oh wait!" She leaped up and grabbed two videotapes off her desk. "I just dubbed these with my dad's old video camera. They're for you."

"For me?" I read the spines. *The Decline of Western Civilization, Part One. Ladies and Gentlemen, The Fabulous Stains.* In Dory's familiar, blocky handwriting.

"Yeah—there's this new girl on my hall, Rachel. She's got this unbelievable bootleg collection. You're going to flip out when you see these movies; they're so killer. *Decline* is, like, a documentary of the whole LA punk scene. And *The Fabulous Stains* has the guys from the Sex Pistols and the Clash. Steve Jones and Paul Simonon are so cute. You'll totally die."

"Cool. Thanks." I couldn't wait to show these to my mom. I wondered if she'd seen them. Dory sat down on the bed.

"Rachel's been getting me obsessed with LA punk—the Germs, Fear. Are you into X?" X. I remembered Gram talking about them.

"Um, I met a guy who is."

"You met a guy who's into X, huh?" Dory raised an eyebrow at me. "New York guy? Tell me more."

"Actually, he's a Gaffney guy. But he's going to school in New York. He works at a record store."

"Okay, so far he's perfect. What's his name?"

"Gram. And it totally sucks, because he lives, like, an hour from Millville, and he's there right now for Thanksgiving, and I'm stuck down here."

"So, call him! Did he give you his number at home?"

"Yeah."

"And you're waiting for . . . ?"

"I don't know!" I rolled over, burying my face in her pillow. "I feel so lame. I'm down here at Grandma's house—"

"So what? Grandmas are cool. He's probably at *his* grandma's. Do you have his number on you right now? Or did you learn it by heart on the plane ride down here?"

"On the car ride to the plane," I confessed. Dory thrust her see-through plastic phone into my hands.

"Do it, dude. Call him."

"Right now?"

"No, next week. Yeah, now!"

I took the phone off the hook, looking away from Dory's hyper stare. Dory was always talking me into doing things I was way too shy to do on my own. She'd just shrug her shoulders and say "I have no pride" and jump right in. And somehow I was always jumping with her. Singing karaoke. Dancing with drag queens. Calling Gram at his parents' house on Thanksgiving.

My hands got slippery with sweat, dialing the number. I cleared my throat, and then cleared it again.

"It's ringing," I reported. Dory gave me the thumbs-up.

"Hello," a woman's voice on the other end of the line said, and I nearly jumped out of my skin. "You've reached the Medleys. Please leave your name, number, and a brief message after the beep. And have a blessed day."

"It's the machine," I hissed, just as the beep smarted my ear.

"Um—hi. This is a message for Gram. Uh, this is Maria, from New York, and I'm just calling to say hi and . . . have a blessed Thanksgiving." I hung up the phone, my face and neck on fire with embarrassment.

"Have a blessed Thanksgiving?"

"It just came out! The machine said to have a blessed day!" I clobbered myself with Dory's pillow. "He's going to think I'm making fun of him."

"No, no. It's totally cool," Dory reassured me. "Wishing them a blessed Thanksgiving—parents love that shit."

"Can I die now?" I said to the heavy down of the pillow.

"Dory?" There was a knock on the door. Dory's mom opened it. "Honey, your dad's packing the car. Half an hour."

"Okay. I'm ready whenever."

Mrs. Mason looked at the floor, at the upended contents of Dory's backpack and suitcase, and then back at Dory.

"Dorothy, this room—"

"I know. I'm cleaning it up," Dory said.

Her mother sighed. "Everything all right, Maria?"

"Yes, ma'am." I sat up.

"She's recovering from crush fatigue," Dory said.

"Hey!" I swatted her arm. Her mom just smiled.

"Ah, understood. Just make sure you get your beauty sleep," she advised. "I have to run and take the casserole out of the oven. You girls have fun catching up." She closed the door behind her.

"Have a blessed Thanksgiving," I called out, and Dory and I both fell back on the bed, laughing.

Thanksgiving stopped being my favorite holiday about three years ago, when my grandmother started inviting all her friends. I guess she got tired of being the minority around my dad and me, who just wanted to watch the parade, eat too much turkey, and fall asleep early. Now we had to dress up and hobnob with the Donninghams and the Spinellis and the Brents, listening to them go on and on about what a beautiful mass it was this year, then gossip about who was getting fat and whose dress was the most unflattering. Dad and I sat across from each other at one end of the long dining room table, chewing our drumsticks and kicking each other under the table when the conversation got particularly dreary. We hadn't said much to each other since I'd gotten off the plane, but I was glad to still have a partner in crime.

"Maria, we hear you're in New York now." Mr. Brent's voice boomed down the table. He was a big wheel at some textile plant in Marietta. "How's the city life treating you?"

"Fine, thanks." I stuffed a forkful of sweet potatoes in my mouth, hoping they'd take the hint.

"Mitchell, we should go up to the city for some Christmas shopping this year," Mrs. Donningham said. "There's nothing like riding down Fifth Avenue at Christmastime. Seeing the big tree at Rockefeller Center."

"Have you been to see any shows yet, Maria?" Mr. Spinelli asked.

"No, sir," I replied politely. "But I—"

"Maria's been very busy with school," Grandmother said, giving me a look that told me to take whatever sarcastic comment I was about to make and nip it in the bud.

"Oh, if you get a chance, you really should see the Disney one they've got now. *Beauty and the Beast*," Mrs. Spinelli said. "It was absolutely breathtaking. Remember that one, Artie?"

"Now, that was cute. We took the grandkids. They loved it." Mr. Spinelli heaped more stuffing onto his plate. "But the one you really have to see is *The Cats*. That's a classic. They've got some real numbers in that one." Mr. Spinelli gave me a wink.

Beneath the table, I felt a tap on my shoe. I looked up at my dad. He nodded and gave me the thumbs-up sign, like he'd seen it, too. I swallowed a laugh and kicked him back.

The guests finally left after coffee and pumpkin pie, and my grandmother retired at her usual nine o'clock bedtime. I found my father sitting in the porch swing out front, drinking a Coors and listening to the crickets.

"Hey, slugger," he said.

"Hey." I sat down next to him. The swing jostled for a second, then got back into its rhythm. The yellow porch light glowed behind us. Across the street, the streetlamp was flickering white through the branches of the willow tree in the yard as they waved in the breeze.

"You warm enough in just that sweater?"

"I can take it." I was wearing one of the thin sweaters Mom bought me at Trash and Vaudeville. "I'm half New Yorker, you know."

"Yup. I know." He sipped his beer. "How is your mother, by the way?"

"She's fine. She's doing really well, actually. She misses you."

"No, she doesn't." He made a noise that was more of a snort than a laugh. I didn't know why I said it, either. We both knew it wasn't true.

"I miss you, though, kiddo," he said. "You know, I can't figure out how to fold a bottom sheet to save my life?"

"Yeah, you're shit at housekeeping."

"Wanna watch that mouth?"

"Sorry." I couldn't help it. Did he really miss me, or did he miss having somebody to keep the linen closet in order? I looked out at the long willow branches swinging gracefully as the breeze picked up again. They looked like slow, dancing arms. I thought about what Nina told me, that my dad had gone to New York all those years ago to be a country singer. The old guitar in our closet must have been his. I wanted to ask him why. Why did he do it in the first place, and why did he quit? But there was something about my dad that made him impossible to talk to. It was like he had this invisible wall around him that absorbed sound. Stupid questions, and sometimes even important ones, never actually got through to him. He would mutter something noncommittal, like "Well, I reckon," or "Probably not, but you never know," or, the worst, "That's a story for another time." Only it was never another time.

My mind wandered to Mom and Travis. I wondered what they were doing for Thanksgiving. If they were eating sushi and stuffed grape leaves and watching *Buckaroo Banzai* on videotape.

"I was thinking." I cleared my throat. "That, um, since I'm down here now, for Thanksgiving, that I could stay with Mom for Christmas."

"No. You're coming home."

"Why? That's not fair. I never get to spend the holidays with Mom."

"Victoria doesn't care about the holidays. Not like your grandmother and I do." He took a long drink of his beer.

"Mom cares. She cares a lot about Christmas." Dad gave me a look. "Why wouldn't she? Anyway, I thought you hated coming down here for the holidays."

"I don't care for the drive, but I like the holiday. It's an important time. It's a time to be with your family."

"Mom *is* my family. You're the one she divorced, not me." At that, my dad gave a heavy sigh, then he got quiet. He took another long sip of his Coors. I knew I'd gone too far.

"Okay, fine, whatever. I'll come back down here. Jesus."

"Watch it."

"Sorry."

I kicked at the porch and sent the swing off its rhythm again. My father planted his feet and steadied it. He pushed with his heels to start the rocking again, but now I kept my feet flat. The chair jerked, refused to glide smooth. I stood up. This game was stupid. I was going back inside.

"So what do you want, anyway?" he asked.

"What?" I stopped at the screen door. The breeze blew again, and I shivered. "What do you mean, what do I want?"

"For Christmas. What do you want for Christmas this year?"

"Oh." I thumbed the latch and looked back at him. He wasn't even looking at me. He stared out at the willow branches and rocked back in the swing. It didn't matter what I said. He'd forget it, like he forgot everything, just like Grandmother said. In one ear and out the other.

"A motorcycle," I told him. I saw a faint smile on his face right before I went back inside, the door slapping shut behind me.

PART
THREE

10

Travis had the TV on with no sound and the stereo going full blast. He sat on the floor with his guitar in his lap, but he wasn't playing it.

"Hey." I dropped my bags. "Where's Mom?"

"Oh, hey. Whoa." He looked over his shoulder. "When did you get back?" His voice sounded thick, like he'd just woken up.

"Just now." Grandmother had called Nina and arranged for her driver to pick me up at the airport.

"Your mom's at—she's at Lee's—he's back in town. You're supposed to meet her. I think she left you a note. Somewhere . . ." His head dropped suddenly, like he was falling asleep. Then he jerked it back up.

"Travis? Are you all right?" I knelt down next to him. He was pale and clammy.

"I'm good." He breathed a snorting breath full of snot. "I've got this cold. Or the flu or something. I'm fine. I'll be fine."

"Do you want me to get you something? I think we've still got some NyQuil from when Mom was sick."

"No, no." He closed his eyes. "No. Maria. Hey. Come here and listen to this for a second."

"I'm right here."

"Are you listening? It's the second Voidoids album. Bob Quine, man. This guy's a . . . this guy's a genius."

Crouched next to Travis, in between the speakers, the genius of Bob Quine was all I could hear. The only lyrics I could be sure of, though, were the ones repeated in the chorus. *Staring in her eyes.*

"He's, uh . . ." I struggled to come up with the right thing to say about the song. "He's got a cool voice."

"No, not the—" Travis cackled a rasping laugh. "Not the singer. That's Richard Hell. Quine's the guitar player. Listen to this solo coming up." Travis reached for the volume knob and cranked it even higher. The guitar around his neck put him off balance, though, and he fell back, almost landing in my lap. The guitar jabbed into my thigh. Travis went limp in my arms, like a bony cat. There was a smell coming off of him, a pungent smell like something poisonous on fire.

"Travis?"

"Sorry, sorry . . ." he mumbled, crawling back to his spot on the floor.

"I think I'd better call a doctor."

"No doctors. I, uh—I don't have insurance. I'll be fine, okay? Just listen to this song with me, Maria. Just for a minute, before you go."

"I don't know if I should leave you."

"I'll be fine. Just listen to this song."

I listened. Travis closed his eyes. The guitars swept and squealed and lifted into the air around us, bright and clean and warm. It was like there was a dark room, but someone had opened a door and you could see that outside it was sunshine, summer.

"It's beautiful," I said. But when I looked back at Travis, his head was tilted against the futon, and he was asleep. I undid the strap and lifted his guitar off him. I propped it up carefully against his amp. Then I went back for Travis. I slid my arms beneath his and pulled with all my strength. I managed to get him up on the futon and lay him out straight. He murmured a little but didn't wake up.

Mom's note was on the kitchen counter, telling me that she had a surprise for me at Lee's, with directions written into a sketch of a bunch of postcards falling out of a mailbox. But I was worried about leaving Travis. I got a glass of water from the kitchen and put it on the floor next to him. I couldn't find any Kleenex, so I left a roll of toilet paper next to the glass. He was sweating, but I was afraid he'd wake up chilled, so I found a clean sheet in the laundry basket in Mom's room and pulled it over him. Just in case, I found the NyQuil bottle in the bathroom and left it with the toilet paper and the water glass. That was everything I could think to do for somebody with the flu. I turned the stereo down and the television off and decided I'd wait for a while, to make sure Travis didn't wake up needing something he didn't have, and find himself all alone.

Mom's note had precise directions on how to get to Lee's loft and, once I was there, how to get in. I had to press the button for L. Kulczek, wait for the door lock to buzz open, then find the freight elevator, get in, shut both grates, hit the red button, and hold it down until I saw the "5" for fifth floor.

Mom met me at the elevator. "I thought you'd never make it! What happened? Was the plane delayed?"

"No, I was worried about Trav—"

"Did you walk down Twenty-Third Street and see the Chelsea Hotel?" She slammed the elevator grate closed behind me. She wasn't listening. "Everybody lived at the Chelsea. Sid and Nancy. Leonard Cohen. Patti. Jim Carroll. Lee! Maria's here!"

Mom's voice rang out as we walked across the loft, our footsteps echoing. The loft was one long room, one side of which was lined with bookshelves and dominated by a giant, brightly colored painting of a pouting blonde. Along the other side of the room, the tall windows made the city outside seem like a living mural. Cars moved along the West Side Highway, the city edged into the river, and, far off, you could see the bridge into New Jersey. It wasn't dark yet, but the lights along the bridge twinkled in the haze.

"Let me see the infamous offspring." Lee stood behind a bar, uncorking a bottle of wine. He wiped his hands on a kitchen towel and clipped toward me, his eyes narrow behind lime-green glasses. He was short, bald, and dressed entirely in black silk.

"My God, Victoria." He gave an exasperated sigh. "Look at her. It's positively sickening."

"I *know*!"

"Tall *and* thin. Mmm." He shook his head, then reached out to rub my arm. "Well, God bless you, honey. Some folks get all the breaks, don't they?" He broke into an abrupt laugh. "Don't look so scared, kiddo! I don't bite." He held out his hand. "Lee Kulczek, at your service."

"Maria." I shook his hand.

"And so shy!" He turned to my mother. "She doesn't get this from you, obviously." Lee put his arm around me. "Your mother and I survived the Jersey Shore together in the seventies. We go back forever."

My mother nodded. "Lee saved me from an overdose of bar bands with saxophones."

"So, girls, who's helping me drink this wine?" Lee wagged his finger at both of us, eeny meeny miny mo.

"Ooh, I am!" Mom held up her hand like a kid in school. Lee went back to the bar.

"Maria?" He held up a wine glass.

I shook my head. "No, thank you."

"My goodness, you don't have to be so polite!" Lee laughed again. He handed my mom a glass of wine.

"She'll loosen up," she said, taking the glass. I wondered what happened to her AA meetings.

"Is it me?" Lee turned a serious gaze to me, his hand to his chest. He mock-whispered, "Am I your first gay man?"

"No," I told him.

"Of course not. Surely you must get a few of those repressed, Tennessee Williams types down there in the South, don't you?"

I shrugged. I'd had to read *The Glass Menagerie* last year for English, but I didn't know what that had to do with gay men. I thought about the gay club I went to with Dory.

"I dunno. We get RuPaul types, though."

At that, Lee roared, a giant, cackling laugh. He walked around the bar, put his arm around my shoulder, and led me to a mirror riveted to the brick wall.

"In that case, come with me, dollface. Your mother wants me to fix you up."

"Work your magic!" Mom called out, settling down on the oversized blue velvet sofa with her wine glass and a thick magazine. "I'll just be over here with Debbie and the latest issue of *Vogue*."

"Now, don't you start with me, Victoria." Lee shot her a look. "She doesn't care for my latest acquisition," he whispered back to me, gesturing to the picture of the pouting woman. "It's an *original Warhol*," he called out to Mom.

My mom muttered something under her breath that sounded like "disco cheesecake."

"Victoria!" Lee stamped his foot. "I have told you time and again: I don't care what you do in the privacy of your own home, but in my presence you are not to refer to Miss Deborah Harry as anything less than the goddess she is."

"Yeah, yeah." Mom waved her wine glass at him.

"What about you, kiddo? Blondie fan?"

"Me?" I shrugged. "I dunno. Aren't they, like, disco?"

"Ach!" Lee held up both hands and walked back to the bar. "Both of you! You say 'disco' as if it's a bad thing." He brought one of the bar stools over to the mirror. "I'm sure your mother's been filling your head with Patti Smith and Lou Reed and all kinds of scary things. Sit," he commanded.

"I like Patti Smith," I protested.

"Of course you do. Your mother would not let you into the house otherwise. Now." Lee put both his hands on my shoulders, studying my reflection in the mirror. "I realize this is a terrible cliché, but not only am I a gay man, I am a gay *hairdresser*." He feigned shock. "I know, right?"

"Mom told me you work with models. She said you were over in Milan or something."

"I was indeed. Models, *ecch*." He rolled his eyes as he ran his fingers through my hair. "In my next life, I'm going to wrestle alligators for a living. It's safer and less stressful." Lee looked back at my mom, then leaned down to whisper in my ear. "I know Vic wants me to set up an appointment for you to have headshots. But I'm telling you now, don't do it. Get out before you get in. They'll eat you alive. In the meantime"—he stood up straight and his voice got loud again—"what are we doing with you? Your mom says you need a new look."

"I do?" I looked at myself in the mirror. My hair was pretty boring. Long and straight. Plain black. Like my dad's.

"Don't take it personally. Everybody needs a new look once in a while." Lee pushed a rolling cart over from the far wall and opened one of its drawers. He took out a cape and snapped it open, fastening it around my neck. "Even the beautiful people like yourself."

I studied my face in the mirror as he combed out my hair. I saw my dark eyes, the shadows beneath them. The long planes of my cheeks. The nose was my grandmother's. Aristocratic, she called it. But my eyes, the way my mouth turned down, those were my father's. As Lee worked, I studied my jaw, my forehead, my ears, looking for signs of my mother. Sometimes I thought we had the same smile. But, searching now, I couldn't find anything of her in me. I couldn't see any way that we were built the same.

Mom was practically bouncing down the street. I had to hurry to keep up with her.

"Okay, for the millionth time, your hair looks so amazing! Isn't Lee, like, a total god?"

"I like it," I said, trying to convince myself. Lee had hacked off a good five inches of my hair and made it all different lengths. Then he took what was left and tousled it all around until it looked like I'd just gotten caught in the wind. Or like I was the runner-up in a contest of people trying to look like that guy from the Cure. I didn't think it was possible, but when I saw myself in the mirror, I actually looked five inches *taller*.

"People are staring," Mom whispered.

"Yeah, because they think I'm Larry Bird."

"No, silly." She whacked my arm. "Because you look like a supermodel! Oh, wait, this is us!" She stopped at the brick building on the corner, sweeping her arms out like one of the girls on *The Price Is Right*. Except the item up for bid was a cartoon sketch. A movie poster.

"Ta-da!" she sang out. "*Rock 'n' Roll High School*! This might just be my favorite movie of all time. Come on." She tugged at my sleeve. "You are so going to freak out over this movie."

We got in line at the ticket booth, the guy in front of us sporting a Mohawk, the two behind with their hair hanging in their eyes and wearing faded Ramones T-shirts.

"Shouldn't we go check on Travis?" I'd been bugging her about him since we left Lee's.

"He's fine," Mom said, rolling her eyes. "He knows what happens when he doesn't take care of himself. Anyway, look, how often do we get to spend girl time together? Like, never. So let's just hang out, enjoy ourselves for once."

"I know. It's just—he seemed really sick."

"Two, please." Mom passed a twenty-dollar bill to the girl at the ticket booth.

"He was, like, passed out when I left. And he was all sweaty, and I think he was running a fever."

"Why are you so concerned about Travis all of a sudden?" She handed me my ticket, looking annoyed. "What are you, his nursemaid?"

"I just—I was kind of freaked out when I left because it seemed like he was pretty bad off, that's all." I followed my mom into the theater, where we took a couple of seats on the aisle.

"Okay. All right." Mom jumped up as soon as she'd sat down. "Will it make you feel any better if I go call Travis? Make sure he hasn't died tragically from a nose cold?"

"Yeah, it would." I didn't see why she was so upset. It was Travis, after all. And he was sick.

"I'll be right back." She squeezed past me, digging in her pocket for change. The lights dimmed as soon as she'd left, and the previews began. Previews for old black-and-white movies. Movies with strange, jumpy edits and subtitles in French.

"He's fine," Mom whispered, back already.

"Good," I replied. But I could tell she was irritated from the way she sat, so stiff, her arms crossed tightly over her chest.

"I didn't mean to keep bugging you about Travis," I whispered to her. "I just thought you'd be worried about him, too."

One of the kids in the Ramones T-shirts shushed us. I sank down into my seat as the movie began, feeling prickles against my neck where tiny hair clippings had fallen into the collar of my shirt. On-screen, a girl in bright spandex cranked the Ramones on the school loudspeaker, and all the kids danced. I couldn't concentrate, though. I couldn't stop thinking that somehow I'd ruined our girl time, that I'd been a worrywart and a bore, and my mom was sick of me.

But then finally, when the evil principal, Miss Togar, came on-screen and tried to shut down the Ramones party, and the girl in the spandex introduced herself as Riff Randall, Rock 'n' Roller, my mom giggled and relaxed in her seat. She leaned over to me and whispered again.

"Remind me to pick up some orange juice on the way home," she said. The kid behind us shushed us again.

"Oh, shush yourself," Mom said over her shoulder, and laughed.

11

Normally Nina's driver was the one waiting on me. But today, he was running late. I stood on the corner, shivering. The music from Citygirls suddenly thumped louder, and I turned to see one of the girls slipping out the door and lighting a cigarette. She stepped to the curb and peered down the street, then stepped back to wait with me beneath the glowing pink awning.

"Hey," she said. "You live upstairs, right?"

"Yeah." I spoke cautiously.

"I've seen you going in and out. That must be so noisy, living up there. Do you guys get any sleep?"

"Sure." I shrugged. "It's pretty quiet once you close the door and everything."

"I'm Shawna, by the way." She extended her hand, and I shook it. Her nails were impossibly long, bright pink, acrylic.

"Maria."

"You waiting on your boyfriend or something?"

"No, just a friend."

"My boyfriend's probably forgot about me." Shawna snorted and took a drag on her cigarette. "I'm supposed to be off, but I was filling in for the girl that takes the money. You'd think you wouldn't get tired, just sitting on your butt, making change. But it's so *boring*." She shook her head. "I'd rather dance."

"Do you, um, do you make good money?" I cleared my throat. "Dancing?"

"Hell, yeah," she said, jumping from one foot to the other to warm up. "I make more money than my boyfriend some weeks, and he's in construction. And at this place, you get medical *and* dental. It's a lady who runs it."

"Oh." I nodded, not knowing what to say. "That sounds like a good deal."

"You thinking about trying out?"

"Me? No way." I laughed, then I stopped, not wanting to insult her. "I mean, I can't dance."

"Honey, you don't gotta be a Rockette. You just shake what you got." She waggled her butt to demonstrate. We both laughed. Just then, Nina's driver pulled up in the limo, honking his horn.

"Gotta run." I waved good-bye. "Nice to meet you."

"Damn, girl! Ride in style!"

There were crowds swarming, lights in the shape of snow-flakes fastened to lampposts, and the taste of peppermint and sugar melting between my teeth. Nina and I walked side by side down Fifth Avenue after a day at the Guggenheim and an early dinner at an expensive bistro. She'd let me borrow a silk dress and a fancy wool overcoat. I felt like someone else. When I caught my reflection floating between the mannequins in the storefront windows, in Nina's coat and Lee's haircut, I hardly recognized myself.

"Have you got any more of those mints?" Nina asked. I reached into my pocket and handed her one of the foil-wrapped mints I'd swiped back at the restaurant.

"Thanks again for dinner," I said. "You didn't have to go all out."

"My pleasure," Nina replied. "You seemed right at home. I didn't even have to tell you which fork to use."

"And did you notice how I kept from spitting on the floor the whole time?"

"Your grandmother would be so proud."

I tucked my hands farther into the coat pockets. A light snow had fallen that afternoon, and Nina laughed when I got so excited over the flurries. We didn't get much snow in Millville. I wondered if we'd have a white Christmas.

"Have you given any thought to your mother's Christmas present yet?"

"A little." I was having a hard time coming up with any good ideas. And I wanted it to be special.

"If you see anything here you think she'd like, let me know," Nina said. "I'll help you pay for it."

"Thanks, but . . ." I looked back at the shops we'd passed. Gucci. Prada. Versace. "I don't think this is exactly—"

"I know." Nina laughed. "Victoria's not exactly one for a Chanel suit."

"I just wish I had more—" I stopped.

"More what?"

"I wish I had more money. I mean, my own money."

"It does go quickly up here, doesn't it?" Nina mused. "Maria,

I realize that your mother—" She sighed. "Listen, just come to me. Anytime you need money. Don't even bother your mother. I'll give you whatever you need, no questions asked. Agreed?"

I nodded, trying to keep up with her quickened pace. I agreed, but that wasn't what I wanted. I didn't want another Grandmother, offering to hand me money anytime I wanted, for whatever I needed, claiming there were no strings attached. When money was involved, strings were always attached. With money came expectations. I had been here before. Once money was invested, some kind of payback seemed inevitable: good grades, or good behavior, or just some indefinable poise—better clothes, unbitten nails—some outward signifier that I was worth the investment. I didn't want to be indebted to Nina. I wanted something else. Like those tiny countries we studied in European history, I wanted autonomy. An uprising. I wanted out from under the expectations. I wanted to prove myself to nobody but me.

I was thinking about how to tell this to Nina when I barely knew how to say it to myself when, in the sea of people coming toward us, I saw a familiar blond bob. It was my grandmother's friend Mrs. Donningham. I almost did a double take.

"Maria? Maria Costello, is that you?" She grabbed my arm and we stopped, clogging the sidewalk artery and forcing the crowd to move around us. Mr. Donningham was a step behind her, his arms full of shopping bags.

"Hello, Mrs. Donningham."

"Well, if this isn't the biggest small town in the world!" Mrs. Donningham caught me in a hasty embrace. "This morning we ran into Mitchell's old business partner having breakfast at the Waldorf. And now here you are! This must be your mother—"

"Pleased to make your acquaintance." Nina deftly shook Mrs. Donningham's hand before I could correct the mistake.

"We're the Donninghams. Mitchell and Doreen. We're friends of Maria's grandmother, down in Atlanta."

"Ah, yes. Mrs. Costello. Do say hello to her for us," Nina said, cool as a cucumber.

"Certainly! We'll—"

"I'm sorry, but we're terribly late." Nina hooked her arm through mine.

"Bye—" I waved as Nina whisked me away, back down the street into the cold specks of freshly falling snow.

"What are we late for?" I asked.

"We're late for not entertaining the Donninghams," Nina said. I laughed as we rushed into the parting crowd.

It was late, but I wanted to go by the record store and see Gram. We'd been talking on the phone, but we hadn't seen each other since the party. Actually, I'd been talking to his answering machine more than I'd been talking to him. He had finals and recitals, and I didn't want to push it. I was afraid I was calling him too much, being a pest. But I wanted to see him again.

"Wow, look at you."

"I know." I was still wearing Nina's coat and the silk dress. "I had to go to a thing."

"What, the opera? Nice hairdo, by the way."

"You like it?"

"Yeah. You don't?"

"I kinda think it makes me look like I've got a . . . giraffe neck or something." I touched my hair self-consciously. "I can't wait till it grows back out."

"Naw, naw, leave it cut. What this ugly old world needs is more of your lovely neck."

A customer stepped up to the counter and handed Gram his stack of CDs. Blushing, I drifted down the aisle to browse the records.

"Looking for something in particular?" Gram called out as the customer walked out the door. Gram and I were alone in the shop.

"Just doing a little Christmas shopping," I said. He came down from behind the counter and walked to the bin where I stood.

"So, uh, you going back to South Carolina for Christmas?"

"Not if I can help it."

He laughed. "Maybe we can get together sometime before you go," he said. "I had a really good time with you at the SSKs."

"Me too." I bit my lip. "How's your tattoo?"

"Totally healed. Check it out." He rolled up his sleeve. The swelling had gone down, and now the letters snaked beneath his skin, fuzzy-edged, inky black. I thought about Travis's tattoo, the one above his heart. I wondered how much it had hurt. I touched the letters on Gram's arm, feeling the faint hairs on his smooth, pale skin.

"Hey, Gram?"

"Yeah?"

"I'm—actually, I am looking for something in particular."

"Shoot." He pushed his sleeve back down.

"Do you know anything about Joni Mitchell?"

Mom knelt next to me at the stereo as I unwrapped the blank tape.

"It's the easiest thing," she said. "Just flip this lever to the left for records, all the way to the right for CDs. Press play and record at the same time, and there you go."

"Thanks." I chucked the tape into the deck and switched the turntable on. "Thanks for letting me use your records, too."

"Use anything you like! I think it's so sweet that you and your friends make mixtapes for each other. This is the girl who gave you the videos, right?"

"Dory, yeah." Mom and I had watched both movies back-to-back one night when Travis was at rehearsal. We ordered a pizza and then made French toast for dessert and nearly made ourselves sick dancing around to X and the Germs after we ate.

"If you're set"—Mom pounced up off the floor like a cat—"then I'm gonna meet Travis. I told him I'd help put up flyers for the show." She grabbed a stack of Xeroxed flyers sitting on the kitchen counter and a roll of tape and shoved them all into her oversized purse. "Are you sure you don't wanna come?"

"I'm sure." I wanted to help them out, but I wanted to make this tape for Dory, too, for Christmas. "I'll meet up with you guys later."

"Definitely." She kissed the top of my head. "Sushi. Or the Moroccan place. We'll call you."

She left, locking the door behind her, and I was there with the stacks of records and CDs. The afternoon sun slanted across the floor; Saturday, and nothing to do but wade through these songs, build this mixtape. I wanted to make the perfect tape for Dory. I wanted it to rise and fall, to put the perfect songs in the perfect order, the way she did. But mostly I wanted to paint this picture for her. This picture of New York, of everything I'd heard since I moved here. Mom's music, Travis's and Gram's, and mine, now. The songs I'd taken as my own, that looped in my head as I walked the streets and rode the subways. The songs that saturated the apartment like another coat of paint, black and white and red and black again and blue, the running motor of guitars, the voices we knew as well as our own. I wanted to paint this picture for Dory to let her know I was okay, that I was over it now, that I had gotten better and I wasn't alone anymore.

I slid the first album out of its sleeve and put it on the turntable. Pressed play and record at the same time, let the needle drop. Patti singing *Jesus died for somebody's sins . . .*

12

My mom was actually jumping up and down on the corner of Bleecker and Bowery, waiting for the light to change. And it wasn't just because it was freezing out and the only warm thing she had on was her Patti Smith jacket.

"Oh my gosh! Okay, can I tell you how totally psyched and proud I am right now?" She put her hands on my shoulders and kept jumping. "It's your first show at CBGBs! Do you have any idea how much this place changed my *life*? Why are you not jumping?!"

So I jumped!

"I know!" I couldn't help but get excited, too. From the second Travis announced that the band had landed a gig at CBGBs, it was like Mom revved into hyperdrive. She circled the date on the calendar and did a countdown, crossing off the days with different-colored markers.

"It's not that big a deal," Travis had insisted after Mom's initial freak-out. "It's a total hole now. And it's just us and a bunch of other crappy bands. It's not like we're opening for the Ramones or anything."

"I know, but . . ." Mom held out her hands like she was describing an elephant. "It's *history*, honey. It's *CBGBs*. It's the first place I ever saw the Ramones. And Patti, and Richard Hell, and Sonic Youth . . ."

The light changed and she grabbed my hand, both of us now jumping and running across the street.

"Vic!" The door guy in a black satin jacket put his arms around my mom, yelling over the music. "Where you been?"

"I've been exiled to Brooklyn! Jimmy, this is my kid, Maria."

"No kidding. Looks more like your kid sister."

"You know I love you forever now, right?" Mom kissed his cheek. "Can we go on back?"

"Of course. Lemme get your hands." Jimmy pressed the backs of our fists with a rubber stamp in the shape of a star. Inside, the room was long and narrow, not nearly ás big as I thought it would be. As we passed the bar, a woman with heavy black mascara and magenta hair recognized my mom and jumped off her bar stool.

"Vic!"

"Hi, Paula!" Mom hugged her. "This is my—"

"Oh my God, Vic," Paula cut her off, her eyes wide. "Did I tell you?"

"Tell me what?"

"I had a beer with Lenny Kaye!"

"Get out."

"For real! Tom took me to see this band, some friend of his, and he was just hanging out at the bar—Lenny Kaye! And he's so fucking cool! He's, like, the coolest guy ever!"

"Hang on, I gotta go meet my boyfriend, okay? But I wanna hear all about it." Mom grabbed my hand. Once we were past the bar, she explained, "Paula's even more of a die-hard Patti fan than I am. I used to see her at the shows back in the seventies. But she's a little, you know, overboard sometimes."

"Who's Lenny Kaye?"

Mom gave me a look. "Uh, Maria? Patti Smith's guitar player?" Mom held her hand to my forehead like she was checking for a fever. "Not to mention the editor of all those *Rock Scene* magazines we were looking at the other night. Remember 'Ask Doc Rock'? I thought you were paying attention."

"I guess I forgot—"

I didn't have time to be embarrassed about forgetting the name of Patti Smith's guitar player. Mom was pulling my hand again, weaving us through people all standing around in clumps, kids with dyed-black hair and messenger bags slung over their shoulders, a collage of punk badges dotting each one, too cool to dance or even jump in place. We pushed past the stage, down a narrow hallway, to a small, graffitied room without a door. The room was packed with guitar cases, amps, drum parts. Slade and Gary sat on a duct-taped bench, and Penny stood with her eyes closed, strumming her guitar, running through the songs.

"Hey, guys," Mom called out. "Where's Travis?"

"Hey!" Penny's eyes snapped open, like she was coming out of a trance. She hugged Mom and then me, her guitar jabbing into my hip. "I'm so glad you guys are here!" Slade got up to shake our hands.

"I think Travis is in the john," Gary said. He nodded at me. "What's up?"

I shrugged. Mom was grabbing at my hands again.

"You *have* to see the bathroom here," she said. "The toilets are notorious."

"Notoriously foul." Penny scrunched up her nose.

"I'm not sure how I feel about a notorious toilet," I confessed.

"Then why don't you go get us some drinks?" Mom suggested.

"Me?" I didn't think I was allowed to do that.

"A vodka tonic for me, and whatever you're having. Guys?" She turned to the band.

"I'll take a Heineken," Gary said.

"Me too," Slade seconded.

"Would you get me a bottle of water?" Penny reached into the pocket of her leather pants. "Here, I have a drink ticket."

"No, don't worry about it—just ask for Theo and say you're with me," Mom said.

"So that's two Heinekens, a vodka tonic, and a water?" I said sarcastically, waiting for somebody to realize that no bartender in the world was going to serve me a bunch of drinks, no matter whose kid I was. I was sixteen, and I looked sixteen.

"And whatever you're drinking," Mom added.

Unbelievable. I slunk out of the room, feeling demoted. The designated waitress. Fine, they'd see how well their little plan worked when the bartender refused to serve me. I waited patiently for the girl filling glasses behind the bar to notice me, then asked for Theo.

"I'm Theo," she said. "What can I do for you?"

"Two Heinekens, a vodka tonic, and a bottle of water," I said. "And a ginger ale."

"Can I see your ID?" she asked.

"My mom told me to ask for you. My mom's Vic—Victoria Costello."

"Vicki! Oh my gosh, is she here?" Theo leaned over the bar. "She totally saved my life. Your mom is the absolute coolest. Hang on, I'll get you your drinks."

The next thing I knew, I was weaving through the crowd again, hands slipping on cold glasses, beer bottles tucked into the crooks of my elbows, bottled water tucked under my chin. When I got back to the dressing room Mom was gone, but the band was happy to relieve me of my beverages.

"Where'd my mom go?"

"Uh, I think she went to look for Travis." Penny thumbed the way to the bathrooms. "Thataway."

I took my ginger ale and Mom's vodka tonic and pushed past loitering punks in the hallway. Even over the racket of the opening band, I heard Mom and Travis before I saw them.

"Fuck that shit, Travis! Fuck you!"

I gasped and drew back. That was my mom, but it was like somebody else's voice coming out of her. Screaming. I watched her shove Travis into the wall, really hard. He kept his arms folded tight across his chest. He was looking straight down at his shoes. I could see his mouth moving, but I couldn't tell what he was saying.

"I ask you for the littlest, for the *tiniest* fucking thing, and this is what I get. What am I supposed to do now, huh?" Mom yelled.

Travis dropped his chin to his chest and mumbled something I couldn't hear.

"And how is that my fault?" she yelled again.

"Hey," I interrupted. My heart was racing. I felt like I had to save Travis. He stood with his back against the wall, pinching the bridge of his nose. I handed Mom her drink. "Here— here you go. Theo says hi."

"Jesus, Vic. You're gonna let her drink like that?"

"It's ginger ale," I said. I wasn't sure why I was defending my mother, but I wanted them to stop fighting.

"Don't tell me how to raise my kid—"

" 'Cause you're doing a bang-up job on your own," Travis muttered.

"I happen to think I'm doing pretty well, all things considered!"

"Guys, I'm standing right here." *All things considered?* What was that supposed to mean? Considering that we got kicked out of the apartment? Considering that I'm such a screwup?

"Come on." Mom grabbed my elbow, spilling ginger ale down my hand. "We'll see you after the show," she called back to Travis.

"Is, um—" I hesitated. Suddenly, for the first time in my life, I felt kind of afraid of my mom. "Is everything okay?"

"Travis is being a dumbass. Typical boys." She gulped her drink. "Fuck it. Hey, it's still gonna be a great show. They're up next—let's go stake out a spot!"

And just like that, she was happy again. Whatever awful thing had happened to make her so angry was suddenly over. I followed my mom as she pushed through to the front of the stage just in time for the opening band to announce their last number and tell us to stick around for Penny Dreadful and the Antics. I pinched my earplugs into my ears and waited. My mom kept talking about the bands she'd seen here and how great they all were, yelling over the music like nothing bad had happened at all.

Finally the band came on, in full regalia: Gary in spiked metal armbands, Slade in silver pants and no shirt, silver glitter dusting his arms and shoulders. Penny's hair was a shock of pink, her black leather pants and vest so tight, she looked like a cross between a parrot and an inverted exclamation point. And then there was Travis.

He walked onstage last, like he didn't even care that it was CBGBs and he had a show to play. His jeans were ripped at the knees, and the sleeves of his black T-shirt were rolled up, showing the pale, carved muscles of his arms. He didn't even bother plugging his guitar in until after the first song had already started. But he was amazing. His guitar rang out and soared across the entire band, across the crowded room, and out into the street. I forgot everything, swallowed whole by the sound of his guitar. I was completely crashed under it, like being pinned beneath a wave but without wanting to come up for air. I imagined that sound covering the entire city, swelling up on the streets and holding everyone still, transfixed from this spell. The notes erupted and dissolved, whines and crashes, stuttering feedback and electric wallop. Mom and I jumped like mad at the foot of the stage, screaming our heads off, going nuts. I tried to catch Travis's eye to let him know that it was working, that the spell was taking hold. But he never saw us. He never even looked down. The entire time, his gaze was fixed on something far away, hovering over everyone. Something that probably didn't exist at all.

* * *

I couldn't stop talking about Travis, even though I got the feeling that Gram didn't really care.

"He's so amazing. I can't even describe it. You have to come to the next show. You would totally freak out."

"I'd freak right out, huh?" Gram smirked.

"Okay, maybe you wouldn't freak out." We were back in his dorm room after meeting up in Chinatown for dim sum. "You're a real musician, so maybe you wouldn't think it was so great. But I was impressed."

"I trust your judgment." Gram flipped through one of his record crates, looking for the next great thing to turn me on to. "He's probably a righteous player. He might well be the second coming of Yngwie Malmsteen, and here I went and missed it."

"Yng—who?"

"Yngwie Malmsteen. Heavy-metal dude. I take it you're not much of a headbanger." He slipped a record out of its sleeve and set the needle on its edge.

"No, I can't say I'm the headbanging type."

"You're into this guy, though, right?" Gram sat back down on the bed next to me as a deep, haunted voice came out of the speakers. The song was familiar, but slower or something. I couldn't put my finger on it.

"I know this song—"

"The Jeff Buckley version, right?"

"Yeah—'Hallelujah'—but this is—who is this?"

"You never heard the original? This is Leonard Cohen." He handed me the cover. A man's face in shadow, lined and sad in a way that reminded me of my mom's Nico record. "Shoot, I had you pegged for a big Leonard Cohen fan when you said you were into Jeff Buckley. Man, I love *Grace*, but the best thing that record ever did was turn me on to Leonard Cohen. Even though, technically, Jeff Buckley's singing the John Cale version of 'Hallelujah.' Which is pretty damn great, too. This is one of those songs you could play on a pair of spoons and it'd knock your socks off."

"A pair of spoons, huh?" I could tell Gram was about to go off on one of his musical raptures again.

"Oh yeah. This dude is *not* fucking around. And now we gotta hear the John Cale version, too—" Gram lunged for the towering stack of CDs on his desk, but I reached out to stop him.

"Hey, wait."

"What is it?"

"You've been jumping up and down, changing the records all night long. Why don't we just let this one play?"

"Good point, there." Gram eased back into his place on the bed. "Sometimes I get so excited listening to music, I wish I had three heads or twelve ears or something. So I could listen to everything at once."

"I know! And then do you ever feel the exact opposite, like you just wanna listen to one song over and over again?"

"Until every note of it becomes embedded in your DNA and you worry that maybe you're going crazy because you've spent an entire hour listening to one three-minute song about twenty times?" Gram nodded. "I know that feeling."

"Sometimes I feel so lazy because it's all I wanna do. Just listen to music. All day, all night."

"That's not lazy," Gram said. "That's love. Why don't you play an instrument?"

"Never learned how." I shrugged. "Except for the recorder in fourth-grade music class."

"That's a start. It's never too late to start. Get you a drum kit or a guitar or something. Save up, go to a pawn shop, get it cheap. Get that guy to teach you how to play."

"Which guy?"

"The one you're so into. Travis—isn't that his name?"

"Travis?" I laughed. "Gram, that's gross. He's my mom's boyfriend. I'm not *into* him."

"You sound pretty into him when you talk about him playing that guitar." Gram fluttered his eyelashes and pitched his voice up into a falsetto. *"And he's so amazing and far out and wonderful when he plays guitar, it's all shooting stars and unicorns . . ."*

"Shut up! I don't sound like that."

"No, but you sound like you're *into* him."

"Gram." I rolled my eyes. "You wanna know who I'm into? I mean, *really* into?" I locked him in a steely stare.

"Do tell."

"Yngwie Malmsteen."

Gram laughed. And then, finally, he kissed me. Kissing Gram was nothing like kissing Brian. There was something sweet about the way Gram kissed. Something that made me want to kiss him all night.

"Maria." He stopped.

"What's the matter?"

"Nothing. I'm just . . ." He exhaled. "I'm nervous as a damn cat around you. I feel like Mr. Smooth talking to you on the phone, but then you come over here and I feel like . . . like I'm still just some fat kid who can't get laid."

"Gram." I wasn't sure what to say. "You're not just some fat kid to me."

"Really?"

"Really."

"Because I want to spend the night with you, but I'm so—" He shook his head. "I'm so jumpy, I feel like it might as well be my first time."

"I sorta—" I laughed nervously. "I sorta feel the same way."

All of a sudden, I felt in over my head. I mean, I wasn't stupid. I was sitting on some college guy's bed, and we were kissing. I knew the next logical step wasn't necessarily breaking out the Scrabble board. But getting laid? I guess I thought we'd stay at the kissing stage at least a little while longer.

"Do you, uh—" Gram cleared his throat. "Do you wanna spend the night? Because I, uh—I got all the stuff—I mean, I've got condoms and, uh—a bunch of condoms."

God, how mortifying. Just the word, "condom." Sex has got to be the most embarrassing thing on the planet.

"Listen, Gram, I can't—I can't really stay out all night. I mean, I live at my mom's and everything."

"Right, right. I understand." He looked down at his hands.

"But that doesn't mean we can't—you know . . ." I felt myself blushing from my ears to my toes. "It doesn't mean we can't keep kissing for a while and see what happens. I mean, if you don't mind. You know, taking your time."

"For you"—he kissed me again—"I'll take as long as it takes."

It was just after one in the morning when I got back to the apartment. I couldn't hear Travis snoring, and his guitar case was gone. I didn't know if Mom was home. I tiptoed into the bathroom and turned on the light. I studied my face in the mirror. Did I look different? Would they be able to tell? Just like that, I wasn't a virgin anymore. It was supposed to be a big deal, everybody always said. It was supposed to be this big, earth-shattering moment that would change me forever. It was a sin, according to my grandmother. Maybe I shouldn't have let it happen. But I wanted it to happen. And, in the end, it was just kind of . . . nice. Gram was nice. In the end, it wasn't anything. I mean, I didn't feel like I had changed. Gram spoke so quietly when it was over, walking with me to the door, helping me put on my coat. Like I'd been in an accident or something. We kissed in the hallway in a daze. But the whole way home, I expected someone to notice. I was sure that someone was going to leap out at me from the shadows. I kept picturing a preacher, like something out of *The Scarlet Letter*, his finger pointing at me, shouting me down, a halo of fire around his head.

I was glad it happened with Gram instead of with Brian. When I was with Brian, the thought of sleeping with him always made me feel kind of sick inside, even in the beginning when I liked him. But being with someone you loved—wait a minute, did I love Gram? I looked at my reflection in the bathroom mirror. Pulled at my hair, pushed at my sullen cheekbones in the dull glass. At least Gram didn't mind the crummy condition of my skin, all broken out and gross. Wait, wasn't I supposed to be feeling some big feeling, instead of thinking about pimples? Wasn't I supposed to be under the spell of some running-through-the-flowers rhapsody?

Maybe I didn't love Gram yet. But I was definitely *into* him.

I opened the medicine cabinet and fumbled through the

dental floss and deodorant, figuring maybe Travis had some anti-zit stuff in here somewhere. When I moved the Bactine, something fell into the sink. My heart sort of skipped when I saw it. I didn't know what it was, exactly, but I'd seen it before. On those cop shows I watched for the sake of the skyline. It was a little plastic bag, smaller than my pinkie, full of white powder. *Drugs.* Fuck. Okay. What was this?

I picked it up. My fingers were trembling. *Just put it back.* I tucked the packet into its hidden corner behind the Bactine. I closed the medicine cabinet and stepped away like it was radioactive. *Maybe I've got it wrong,* I thought. *Maybe it's ... some weird kind of aspirin.* But it looked like it always did on TV. It looked like it did in the "Just Say No" brochures they gave us in health class. *Okay. Okay.*

I walked out of the bathroom. I walked around the kitchen table. I was pissed. *I'm the teenager, here. Somebody else is supposed to find* my *drugs.* I thought about my mom, always hyper. Did it make you hyper? I thought about Travis, so sick after Thanksgiving, like he was on fire. It had to be his. Did Mom know? What would she do when she found out?

She wasn't going to find out. I went back into the bathroom and yanked the medicine cabinet door open. I took the packet out of its hiding place and threw it in the trash. *Done. Problem solved.*

No, that's no good. That's worse. It's right there in the trash can for everyone to see. I fished it out of the trash, opened it over the toilet, and watched the white powder fan out and hit the water. I tossed the plastic Baggie in after it and flushed. When the tank refilled, I flushed again for good measure. Now it was really done.

I looked at myself in the mirror again. Pulled my hair away from my face and exhaled. Would Travis be angry with me? Would he go into withdrawal, get sick? How much did those drugs cost? Would Mom still find out? Why was Travis doing drugs in the first place? How did he get them? Somebody in the band? Probably Gary. I didn't like that guy from the moment we met. Next time I saw the band, I'd tell Penny they needed to find a new drummer. Maybe I'd tell Gary myself.

"You asked for it, kiddo," I told my pale reflection. "No more kid stuff now."

13

The phone was getting sweaty in my hand. Meanwhile, this conversation was going nowhere.

"Your grandmother already bought you a ticket," Dad repeated. "It's next week. You could've at least said something sooner."

"Can't she cancel it? I told you at Thanksgiving that I wanted to spend Christmas with Mom." I was determined to stand my ground on this, even though the thought of the inevitable Angry Phone Call from my grandmother was already giving me the shakes.

"Maria." Dad sighed. I could tell he was giving up. "Come or don't come, but we're not canceling the ticket."

"Do what you want, but I'm spending Christmas here." I hoped that it would work like it always did. That if I was quiet, and patient, and showed that I wasn't going to throw a temper fit, he would quietly concede.

"You do what you want," he echoed my own words back to me. "I'm late for work. I love you, Maria."

"You too, Dad."

I hung up the phone. Travis walked into the kitchen, yawning. His black shirt hung open, unbuttoned.

"You were out late," he mumbled, opening the fridge.

"So were you."

Travis peered at me as he drank out of the milk carton.

"That's disgusting," I said. "We've all gotta drink that, you know."

He took his time putting the milk back in the fridge. "I had rehearsal last night," he said. "What's your excuse?"

"I was hanging out with a friend of mine." I busied myself taking the clean coffee mugs out of the drying rack and putting them in the cabinet. "Is there some law against hanging out?"

"What friend? That guy from the record store?"

"Yeah. So?"

"I figured." Travis opened the fridge and closed it again. "And what are you gonna do when that fat slob knocks you up?"

"He is not a fat slob, and I'm not—" I stopped. *Wow, could he tell?* "You're sick." I stormed out of the kitchen, but the apartment was so small, there wasn't really anywhere to storm to. I paced around the futon, tearing through the clean laundry that sat half-folded, looking for my good sweater.

"You think we don't know what you're doing?" Travis called out.

"We?" I spun around. "You're not my father." I yanked the sweater over my head.

"If your mom was here right now—"

"She'd probably be totally cool with it. Besides, you think I don't know what you're doing?"

"What are you talking about?"

"Travis." I looked at him. His pale chest beneath his black shirt. The tattoo over his heart. His dark brow. "Just get off my case, okay?" I grabbed my coat, slung my backpack over my shoulder, and walked out.

"This gift is neither romantic nor imaginative, but it's practical." Nina handed me a slender box wrapped in red foil, tied with a green ribbon.

"Nina, I didn't—" I stammered. "I didn't get you anything."

"I didn't expect you to." Nina walked briskly through the living room, closing the blinds against the sharp setting sun.

"But I should have. I don't know why I didn't."

"Maria, I happen to be that woman who has everything. Now, stop apologizing and open your gift."

I slid the ribbon off and ripped the red foil. Inside the box was a black leather-bound book stamped with gold letters. MANHATTAN DIARY. I flipped open the pages. It had everything. Next year's calendar. A day planner. Maps of the entire city. The subway lines and bus routes.

"Wow—Nina, thank you—"

"It's a trifle." Nina waved her hand. "But I think you'll find it useful. The first step to being successful is being organized. And knowing which way you're going always helps. Now"—she put on her overcoat, the one with the fur collar—"I thought that for our last evening before the holiday, we'd start at Lincoln Center—" Her cell phone rang. "Hold that thought."

I tucked the diary into my backpack. I liked having it there.

It made me feel like the next year was definite. Decided. I was staying. I was becoming a real New Yorker. I had to come up with something really great for Nina. Maybe I could get her a record. Some opera music, something classical.

"Hold on—just hold on a moment. Maria"—Nina held her hand over the phone receiver—"have you seen your mother today?"

My heart jumped into my throat. "No. Why?"

Nina shook her head. "Anthony, I'm coming right over. No, don't—Anthony, wait for me." She flipped the phone closed. "Maria, get your coat." Her heels clicked against the hardwood floor and I rushed to catch up.

"Where are we going?"

"Back to Brooklyn."

Nina's driver made it over the bridge in record time. He pulled up in front of Citygirls and we got out. Nina went right up to the club and walked in the front door. I hesitated. She didn't wait for me.

When I walked inside, Nina was already arguing with a short, dark-haired guy in a tracksuit. Sitting on a stool by the door to the rest of the club was a shaved-bald black guy, built like a bodybuilder, reading *El Diario*. The girl I'd met before, Shawna, stood by the counter with a duffel bag over her shoulder.

"Look, I'm sorry." She held up her hand, her bright nails waving. "But I been here since last night, I got my sister and all her kids coming for Christmas, and I can't work another shift—"

"And we don't expect you to," Nina cut her off curtly.

"Ricky said last time he seen her was night before last, and she cut out early then, too," the tracksuit guy said. "That's two days, Nina. And it's the third time it's happened."

"All right. Anthony, let's have this conversation in your office." She looked at me. "Maria, you wanted to earn some money. Shawna, show Maria how to run the register."

Anthony, the guy in the tracksuit, opened the door to the club for Nina. The music shuddered as the door opened, blasting out loud, then fading again as it closed. I caught a glimpse of a girl wearing nothing but bikini bottoms, and I turned my head. For the first time, I looked around and noticed where I was standing. The room was small, just an entryway. There was a chrome-edged counter with a strand of tinsel hastily taped to it. There was a cash register and, behind the counter, a closet with a few coats hanging up. The guy on the stool looked up from his paper, sized me up, then went back to reading, nonplussed.

"You ever run a register before?" Shawna asked me.

"No."

"It's simple. Same price for everybody. Ricky checks IDs, so don't worry about that. If you want to open the door for change"—she pressed a button, and the cash drawer flew open—"it's here. Tony keeps more small bills in the back if you run out, but if he's tied up, you can just ask one of the girls. They're always happy to go home with twenties instead of a big wad of ones. Coat check—here's the tickets. You put this half on the hanger, give this half to the customer." She took a hanger from the closet and demonstrated. "Don't worry, it's always slow at Christmas. And if you need any help, you can ask Ricky." She motioned to the guy with the paper. "He's Dominican. You speak Spanish?"

191

"A little French, but—"

"Don't worry about it." She held up her hands in a flurry. "His English is getting way better. Listen, I gotta go catch the train—good luck, okay?" With that, Shawna bolted. And all of a sudden I was working the coat check at Citygirls. Just me and Ricky.

"Hey," I said. "I'm Maria."

"Hey." He smiled broadly, showing a gold-capped tooth. "Ricky."

"So." I took my coat off and climbed up on the stool behind the register. "I guess it's, uh, kind of a slow day, huh?"

"Yeah." He chuckled, turning the page. "Too cold for titties."

I found a copy of *Rolling Stone* stuffed into a low shelf behind the counter. It was a few weeks old, but I hadn't read it. I opened it up and flipped through, but I couldn't concentrate. I was scared to death of having to actually talk to some guy who was coming into a bar to look at half-naked women. And I was wondering what was going on between Nina and Anthony, and why Nina so desperately needed to know where my mother was.

I'd been sitting behind the counter at Citygirls for a good half hour when she burst through the door. My mom.

"Ricky, hey! Where's—" She saw me and stopped.

"Maria—"

"Mom—"

Her face hardened. She turned back to Ricky.

"Where's Nina?"

She flung open the door to the club. She wasn't waiting for an answer.

"So I guess we need to talk." Mom sat down at the kitchen table. Her eyes were ringed black with mascara smudges.

"I guess we do." My voice sounded flat. I hooked my feet around the rungs of my chair. The teakettle whistled. Mom got up to turn off the burner.

"So I work at Citygirls." She held up her hands. "Now you know."

"I don't care," I told her. "You run a register and take guys' coats. Big deal." Mom set the tea in front of me. "You didn't have to lie about it."

"I didn't want you to think . . ." She sat down and wrapped her hands around her mug. "It's embarrassing, that's all. I had a good job at Nina's boutique, but she closed it, and when she offered me this—" She shook her head. "I needed the money. Don't tell your grandmother, okay?"

"No problem." That was an easy promise.

"Or your dad."

"I won't. Don't worry."

"Speaking of Nina, how long have you two been palling around?" She looked at me with hard eyes. "While we're on the topic of lying."

"She's teaching me—"

"Teaching you what? How to do my job?" Mom snapped.

"It wasn't like that. And why weren't you there, anyway? They said you hadn't shown up in two days—"

"Hey, I'm still the mother here, okay? I told you, I don't want Nina teaching you anything, least of all how to run a strip club."

"She's not teaching me anything about strip clubs. She's been teaching me about art and architec—"

"What in the hell does Nina Dowd know about art?" Mom snorted. She waved her hand, slicing the air. "Forget it. After the holidays, I'm gonna get you in over at the public school. I should never have let this happen. Fun and games are over, okay?"

"Mom—"

"Maria. Look at me. This isn't about me and Nina. This is about your education. I know school's a drag. But I don't want you throwing your whole life away just because Nina shows up in her limo and takes you to her penthouse. You think she's gonna introduce you to people, help you out—it's bullshit. Utter bullshit."

"I didn't ask her to introduce me to anybody," I insisted. "I don't care about her rich friends or whatever. I don't need her help."

"That's what you think now. But you just wait. She'll suck you into her whole psycho society scene, and next thing you know, you're trying to live up to somebody else's . . ." She waved her hand, trying to come up with the word. "Look, Maria, when Nina decides to anoint you with her friendship, it might seem really great at first, but, trust me, you scratch the surface and you'll find a whole world of . . ." She stopped, swallowing hard. "Just don't scratch the surface, okay?" Mom shook one of her cigarettes out of its pack and lit it. "Take it from me, kiddo. I dropped out of school, too. So, look around and think about it. You really wanna end up like me, working for some crazy old broad at her dead husband's strip club?"

"You're doing okay."

"Pfft, yeah." She exhaled, laughing. "I'm doing just *great*."

"Anyway, Nina's not crazy," I said softly.

"Whatever she is, I told you I didn't want you hanging around with her, and I meant it." She stood up, raking her free hand through her hair. "I'm going to go lie down for a while. I've got a headache."

"Mom—" There was more that I wanted to say. I wanted to tell her that Nina was only trying to help. I wanted to tell her that, despite whatever happened between them, whatever the reason was that they weren't friends anymore, Nina really was teaching me. She had shown me so much already; I wouldn't know about Jean-Luc Godard or Edward Hopper or George Gershwin without her. I wanted to tell her that I'd still be stuck at Prince, with the kids making their jokes, calling me Beverly. But her eyes were so dark. Her cigarette was already forgotten in her fingers, the ash growing long and finally falling to the kitchen floor.

"Later, kiddo." She kissed the top of my head. "That's enough drama for one day."

There wasn't much time for us to get together before Gram had to go back to Gaffney for Christmas. He met me on Canal Street after class, at the big Pearl art store. He wandered the aisles with me, singing along to the songs on the overhead radio, while I filled my basket with brushes, paints, pencils, erasers, ink pens, and sketchbooks.

"When am I finally gonna get to see some of this top-secret art you're making?" he asked.

"Oh, I dunno." I picked out an inexpensive box of pastels. "When it's ready."

Okay, I admit, I got myself into a bit of a pickle, here. When I invited Gram to come shopping, I neglected to mention that I wasn't shopping for me. I thought I'd get Mom some new art supplies for Christmas. But before I even said anything, Gram assumed that I was buying all this stuff for myself. Now he was asking me about my portfolio, and I was lying through my teeth.

"Do you ever sculpt? Or is it all painting and drawing?"

"It's mostly, um, the painting and drawing."

"You should draw me sometime. Lookit!" He struck a pose in the aisle, putting his fist to his chin like *The Thinker*. I laughed.

"I know what you're gonna say." He stood up straight, smoothing his curly hair. "I should model. I get that all the time."

"Come on, sexy." I looped my arm through his. "Let's get you outta here before some nice girl tries to make you her muse."

"Ooh, I could be a*mus*ing." He waggled his eyebrows at me, waiting for a laugh.

"Not with that joke."

Outside, the sun was going down, and the street was packed with rush-hour cars honking and edging each other's bumpers. Gram and I wove through the traffic, hand in hand, our breath clouding the cold air. We walked farther downtown, to the Brooklyn Bridge, and walked halfway over it. At the midpoint, Gram pulled me from the stream of commuters hurrying across the bridge, their faces buried in their scarves. We turned back to see the city, the lights coming on against the gray dusk. The wind swept off the East River, icy and stern. I shivered, and Gram held me close, wrapping me in his oversized coat.

"You're so warm," I said.

"Us fat dudes have our advantages." He held me tighter and I laughed. It was so beautiful, looking out over the water, at the whole city, being there with Gram. Standing on the bridge felt bigger than life, like we were characters in a movie. Like the city was moving all around us, all the people, the cars, the lights, and we were part of it, but we were floating above it, too.

I had to tell him that I'd lied to him. I thought about my mom lying about working at Citygirls. Well, not lying, exactly, but keeping it a secret. If I just came out and told Gram that I'd made it all up, that I wasn't really an artist and I didn't go to Pratt and I lied because I liked him so much and I wanted to be his friend, to be close to him, he would understand. Wouldn't he? We were so close now. I had to tell him. It was so perfect here, on the bridge, the two of us together. He probably wouldn't even care. And with the art supplies, shopping for my mom, he might even think it was funny.

"Maria—"

"Gram, I—" We spoke at the same time.

"Go ahead," he said.

"No, mine's longer. You go first."

"I wanted to give you something." He reached into his coat pocket. "I wasn't sure if it was too soon. You know, to get you something for Christmas."

"Same here." I'd brought a present for him, just in case, but I felt weird about it, too. I wasn't sure what the protocol was, how long you were supposed to be dating someone before you exchanged gifts. I figured if he had something for me, great; if not, well, it was just a book that Mom gave me, from a box she was unpacking a few weeks before. A copy of the country music singer Waylon Jennings's autobiography, entitled simply *Waylon*.

"Do you want this?" She tossed it over to the futon, where I sat reading an article Nina had given me on Grace Hartigan, a painter whose work we'd just seen.

"Waylon Jennings?"

"Your father gave it to me." She rolled her eyes. "I guess because Lenny Kaye was the cowriter. But, I mean, seriously. I was like, I know I'm a Patti completist, but Waylon Jennings? Sometimes your dad is so weird."

"Yeah, he's . . ." I trailed off, not in the mood to defend my dad or to agree with my mom. I started to give the book back, but I figured Gram might like it.

"It's not much." He pulled a small box out of his pocket. My heart thudded. Jewelry. This was terrible. He'd gone and gotten me something expensive, and all I had for him was a book. Paperback, no less.

"Oh!" I tore the paper off and was instantly relieved. It was a tape.

"You wanted to know when you could hear some of my music. Well, there it is," Gram explained. "It's this jazz ensemble that I play with for school. I know, it's not too exciting, but—"

"No, no, it's perfect."

"I do my best Thelonious Monk. I know, it's not what you're into, but it's the only thing recent I had on tape."

"Stop apologizing. It's great." I kissed him. "I have something for you, too."

"You didn't have to get me anything."

"It's just a little something." I unzipped my backpack and handed him the gift. "I thought you'd be into it." He tore the paper off.

"Waylon Jennings! Right on! Man, I've been wanting to read this. Thanks!" He kissed me and tucked the book into his coat pocket. He kissed me again and held me tight.

"I guess I oughta go," he said finally. "I gotta get to work."

"I wish you didn't have to work tonight."

"Me too. Especially since I gotta be at LaGuardia at seven in the morning to catch my plane." He shrugged. "But what're you gonna do? Gotta make ends meet up some which-a way."

"I wish you were staying here for Christmas."

"I wish I was, too." He brushed my hair away from my eyes. "When I get back, I'm gonna make some time for us. I promise. We're gonna go out on some serious dates, you and me."

"Yeah?"

"Yeah. And, uh, I was thinking you could come over and spend the night again."

"I was thinking about that, too." I had been thinking about it. But I wasn't sure I was ready to do it again.

"I'm gonna be thinking about you tomorrow morning when I'm reading about Waylon on the plane."

"I hope it's good."

"Doesn't matter." He kissed me again. "It's from you. That's good enough."

14

Mom and Travis slept late, so instead of Christmas morning, we were having Christmas afternoon. Travis was on his second cup of coffee, holding his head like he was hungover. It was my turn to open my present from Mom. I tore the paper off. It was a heavy black box with silver latches and a handle on the side.

"What is it?" I asked.

"Keep opening! You'll see!" Mom reached over and flipped the latches. I took off the lid. It was a record player.

"Just for you! It's an antique, but I listened to it in the shop, and the sound is still really awesome. I figured you could keep it in your bedroom—"

"The stereo's already in my bedroom." I laughed.

"I mean, your bedroom at home."

"My—" I stopped. Oh, of course. At home. At my dad's.

"I just mean, when you go home for a visit!" Mom said quickly, her hands fluttering. "It's cool, right? You don't already have one, do you? See, this way you can play your records in your bedroom and you don't have to worry about your dad giving you a hard time about all that rock-and-roll music."

"I don't have any records."

"Well, not yet! Everybody's gotta start somewhere." Mom reached into her bathrobe pocket. "Here, open this one next." Mom handed me a small white envelope with one of her drawings on the outside. A sketch of the city skyline in black, with fireworks bursting in color overhead. This was what I was used to. A card at Christmas, handmade, with a little money in it. Sometimes five. Sometimes a crumpled ten. Once or twice, twenty dollars. The drawing on the card was always the best part.

"Two presents? This is way too much."

"No, no, it's Christmas! Open it! Open it!" Mom was jumping up and down again. "Anyway, this is more of a New Year's present. And it's a present for me, too."

I opened the envelope, careful not to tear the drawing. Inside were three tickets. Patti Smith. Bowery Ballroom. New Year's Eve.

"We're all going!" Mom plopped down on the floor in front of me. "You and me and Travis! And then, after the show, we stay up all night, and then on New Year's Day, we go to the all-day poetry reading at St. Mark's Church. Patti comes over and reads there, and sometimes Jim Carroll and all kinds of cool people—you're so going to freak out!"

"I can't wait!" I hugged her. "Thanks, Mom!"

"I'm serious!" She pulled out of my embrace, shaking her head. "Seeing Patti live is gonna blow your mind. We're gonna have such a blast! I'm so glad we're going together!" She clapped her hands, surveying the torn paper on the floor beneath the two-foot tree we'd balanced on top of the TV set. "Is that everything? Is it time for Christmas brunch?"

"I think we passed brunch about four hours ago." Travis cackled.

"Travis hasn't opened mine yet." I slipped the package out of its hidden spot beneath the tree.

"I didn't get you anything," Travis said.

"That's okay. I didn't expect you to." I handed him the present.

Travis set down his coffee mug and ripped into the record I'd bought for him at Gram's shop. "No way," he murmured. "This is awesome. How'd you know?"

"I remembered that time at rehearsal. When you were talking about her."

"What is it?" Mom craned her neck. "Joni Mitchell?" She laughed. "Maria, why in the world would you buy Travis a Joni Mitchell record?"

"Because I like Joni Mitchell," Travis said, sliding the record out of its sleeve.

"You do?" Mom raised her eyebrows.

"Yeah." Travis inspected the vinyl for scratches. "I've told you that. My mom used to listen to Joni Mitchell all the time."

"You didn't tell me that," Mom insisted. "How did she know that and I didn't?"

"I guess it's sorta like an inside joke." Travis shrugged. He handed me the record. "Here. Let's try out your new turntable." I put the record on while he knelt down to find an outlet for the plug.

"We're not putting that on," Mom announced.

"Why not?" Travis sat up, dusting his hands on his pajama pants.

"Because I say so." Mom laughed, incredulous. "Because I'm not listening to any of that hippie-dippy, *Ladies of the Canyon* bullshit. That's why not." She turned and yanked the turntable plug out of the wall.

"Vic. Geez. Don't be a drama queen." Travis laughed and bent down to put the plug back in. Mom snatched up a handful of wrapping paper from the floor and stomped off to the kitchen. I heard the garbage can lid lift and slam down again. Travis put the needle down on the record. He turned the volume up a little and we heard fast acoustic strums.

"This thing does have pretty good sound," Travis commented.

"I'm serious, Travis." Mom reappeared, standing over us. "I don't want to hear that hippie crap."

"Vic, it's really good."

I chimed in. "My friend Gram says it's a really underrated—"

"Okay, then, you know what? Fine. Spend Christmas with your friends and your little inside jokes and whatever." My mother's mouth was pinched tight. She turned on her heel, went into the bathroom, and slammed the door.

"Don't worry. She's just in a mood." Travis got up. He knocked softly on the bathroom door. I studied the album cover. The lyrics were printed inside. I liked it. The music wasn't punk or anything, but the lyrics were good. Like poems. I read along with the song until I heard something crash. I stood up and saw Travis following Mom into the hallway.

"Well, somebody did! And it probably wasn't her!" Mom shouted at him. Travis rubbed the back of his neck, looking at his feet.

"Vic, calm down."

"Is this what it's gonna be about now? Everybody just come on in, mooch off Victoria. I had to work hard for—"

"Oh, really? You worked hard?" Travis said.

"Don't start." She gave him a warning look. "I'm the only one working around here, and everybody thinks they can just walk in and help themselves! Well, this was not the deal! This was never the deal!" she screeched.

"Calm dow—" He put his hand out to touch her. She batted him away.

"I'll calm down when you tell me why you thought you could take my shit and I wouldn't even notice—"

"Mom—" I couldn't believe that was me talking. My voice was tiny. "Mom."

"Maria, not now, okay? This is between me and Travis."

"Mom, I think—"

"Maria, just shut up, okay! Just everybody shut the fuck up for five minutes! And turn this goddam hippie music off!" She brushed past me, to the record player. There was a violent scratching noise and then silence. Mom stood there, triumphant over the record as it slowed to a stop. Travis kept rubbing the back of his neck. I felt my throat closing tight around whatever it was I thought I could say.

"That's better," Mom said. But it wasn't better. The quiet in the room was seething. It was a false quiet, like there really was some noise, something loud and horrible, the teakettle screaming, some wailing feedback, a deafening roar that we were all pretending not to hear.

"Mom." Me, again. "It's my fault." But she was staring at Travis, not even hearing me. "Mom?"

"Maria, sweetie, I swear to God. Will you quit with the mom-mom-mom business? You're like a goddam broken—"

"It's got nothing to do with her." Travis put his hand out in front of me, the way you do when you're slamming on the brakes and you don't want your kid to go flying through the windshield. "Whatever it is you think—"

"I took it," I interrupted. "It was me. I'm sorry."

"What?" My mother just stared at me. This wasn't like with my dad, where you could tell he was mulling things over, working it out in his mind. This was more like seeing a wave coming toward you, building. Knowing you couldn't swim away before the crash. *Somebody say something. Why wouldn't she say something? Why couldn't I? Somebody, do something. Anything.*

"What did you say?" she repeated.

"I said it was me. I took your . . . I took your stuff."

"Okay. Then." Mom swallowed. "Now would be a good time for you to give it back."

"I can't."

"You can't?"

"I flushed it down the toilet."

"Of course you did." She shook her head. "Are you covering for him? You are, aren't you?" She looked at Travis. "You think I can't tell? I know you." She looked back at me. "Get out."

"What?"

"Did I stutter? Get. The fuck. Out."

"Vic—come on, it's Christmas. It's freezing out," Travis said. "Everything's closed. Where is she supposed to go?"

"She's got plenty of places to go. She's got her hippie friends and her rich old lady uptown."

"Mom—" I felt a tear slide out of my eye.

"Victoria, let's just chill out for a second, here—"

"No, she needs to learn. You think you can waltz in here . . ." My mother kept her eyes locked on me. "You barge in, you set up camp, you act like you're princess of the whole damned world and the rules don't apply to you. You just take. You take advantage of me. And you expect me to take care of you because your boyfriend broke up with you and you had some little meltdown. Well, guess what, kiddo. Life is full of little meltdowns. You expect me to treat you like a princess? You got me confused with your dear old dad. I'm not somebody you just take from. You understand me? You stole from me; you pay the price. The free ride is over. Get out."

"Victoria, you're outta your mind." Travis stood between me and my mother. I backed away.

I turned and looked around the room. At the things that were mine. It felt like slow motion. Packing the bag. The two of them somewhere far off in the background. Two voices, coming in and out.

"Victoria, take back what you said."

"I didn't say it to you, I said it to her."

"Just because your dad and your stepmom were creeps doesn't mean you can walk all over—"

"You're choosing her over me, aren't you? I can't believe this. You're taking her side over mine."

"Vic, I'm on both your sides."

"You know, maybe you should get out, too."

"Hey, I've paid my share of the rent—"

"The bare minimum. That's all you ever do."

I pulled my old baggy jeans over my flannel pajamas, gathered my clothes, stuffed as much as would fit into my backpack, and laced my bare feet into my boots as fast as I could. My eyes were so blurred with tears, I couldn't see to find my socks.

"*That's not fair. Anyway, this isn't about me. You can't kick your own daughter out on Christmas Day.*"

"*Don't tell me what I can or cannot—*"

"*I won't let you.*"

"*Of course you won't. Because you're on her side.*"

"*This isn't about sides. And you need to calm down. For your own sake—*"

"*You're concerned for my health? How sweet. Is this your thing now, huh? Peace and love and how's your blood pressure? Listen, why don't the two of you go out and have your own little fucking hippie Christmas somewhere. Get yourself one of those tofu turkeys and dance around the maypole—*"

"*Vic, what the hell are you talking about?*"

The bedroom door slammed. I zipped my bag. Travis stood outside the bedroom door, knocking softly.

"Vic, don't be like this. We love you." From inside, Mom's clock radio came on. She cranked it loud, but instead of punk music, it was that Paul McCartney Christmas song. The one that goes *Simply having a wonderful Christmastime.* Travis rolled his shoulders back and sighed. He walked down the hallway, shaking his head at me.

"Maria, seriously." Travis took my backpack. "Relax. You're not going anywhere. She's just in a mood."

"Some mood."

"She'll be over it in five minutes. Christmas is hard for her. You know. She had a bad time growing up, with her stepmom and all."

"Yeah, well, I'm not exactly having a real cool time growing up right now." I took my backpack back from him and headed for the door.

"Where are you going?" He reached out to grab my arm. I dodged him.

"Doesn't matter."

"It matters to me." We stood by the door. He grabbed me and hugged me. I didn't want to go. But my hands were shaking now. I was angry. *Screw it.* She wanted me gone? I was gone. She was right—I had places I could go. I didn't have to hang around here and take it.

I pulled out of Travis's embrace, but he held on to my arms. He looked like he was about to cry, too. Then he pulled me back in to him and kissed me on the mouth.

"Travis! Stop!" I jerked away.

"Sorry—sorry—I'm sorry," he stammered. "Maria—"

I ran out.

My feet were freezing. I finally found a phone booth and closed myself inside it. Gram was down in Gaffney. I dialed Nina's cell phone. I knew she was up in Connecticut with her half sister for Christmas. But she told me to call if there was an emergency.

"Hello?"

"Nina, it's Maria."

"Merry Christmas, Maria. How nice to hear from you. How's your holiday going?"

"Um. Not so great." I was trying not to cry. "I had to leave Mom's. We kind of had a fight. But I don't know where to go."

On the other end of the line, I heard Nina sigh.

"I'll call my doorman as soon as we hang up. He'll let you

into the apartment. Put your things in the guest room and make yourself at home. I'll be back first thing in the morning."

"I don't want to be a bother," I said. "Just tell me where to go."

"Maria, talk sense," Nina snapped. For a minute, she sounded like my grandmother. "You aren't a bother, and I just told you where to go. My apartment. Take a cab if you need to; I keep one hundred dollars in small bills in my silverware drawer. The one next to the refrigerator."

"Are you sure it's okay?"

"I'm only surprised it didn't happen sooner."

Nina's place without Nina was big and empty and lonesome. I couldn't imagine how she lived there alone. I kept walking around, listening to my own footsteps. I looked in the fridge— it was full of gourmet stuff, olives and pâté and expensive cheese—but I wasn't hungry. Even though we never had made it to brunch.

I watched the cold, slanting sun set over Central Park. I kept thinking Nina would come back early, knowing I was alone here in her apartment. But she didn't show. I thought about calling Dory. Thought against it. She'd probably tell her parents, and they'd tell Grandmother, and she'd tell Dad. And I couldn't talk to either of them, not right now. Not after I'd called them first thing this morning and told them how everything was going just swell. I thought about calling Gram. It was long distance to Gaffney, but Nina could afford the charges.

"Medley residence." He picked up on the second ring.

"Gram?"

"Maria?"

"Yeah. Hey."

"Hey yourself." There was an odd silence. "What's going on?"

"I, uh—I missed you and I wanted to call and say merry Christmas. That's all."

"Oh. Merry Christmas to you, too. Did you . . . did you have a good one?"

"Um." I laughed, nervous. Why did I feel like I was interrupting him in the middle of something? "It's been pretty cruddy, actually. Me and my mom got into a fight and I left."

"Wow."

"I'm staying at a friend's right now."

"Are you with that guy?"

"What guy?"

"Maria." I heard Gram exhale hard, seven hundred miles away in Gaffney. "That guy, the guitar player. Your mom's boyfriend."

"Travis?"

"He came into the record shop the other night, right before I left to come down here. He told me about you. He told me you're only sixteen years old. You're an eleventh grader."

I sank down onto Nina's big white couch.

"Gram—"

"I didn't believe him. I didn't think you'd lie to me, after all this time. After—the time we spent together. You wouldn't lie. So why would he say such a thing?"

For a horrible moment, I couldn't say anything. I couldn't make any words come out of my mouth. It was so quiet. I didn't know how to tell him. I didn't know where to start.

"I wanted to tell you."

"Jesus. Maria."

"I didn't mean—"

"Aside from the fact that I could go to *jail*—"

"Nobody's going to—"

"You lied to me. You made me look like an idiot. And now I've got some guy breathing down my neck who knows where I work—"

"He doesn't know anything about us! I didn't—"

"It doesn't matter now. Maria, I really care about you a lot, but . . . let's face it. That dude's in love with you, and you're in love with him."

"No, I'm not! I'm not in love with Travis! He's—he's—" I couldn't believe this. *Travis? Why in the hell would I be in love with Travis?* But when I closed my eyes I could still feel his lips against mine. A nauseous wave lapped against the back of my throat.

"You reckon you'll ever talk about me like you talked about him the night you saw him play guitar?" Gram asked. I had to close my eyes. Travis, of all people. My mother's boyfriend. *Try not to throw up on Nina's couch. Can you at least keep it together enough not to puke on the couch?*

"It doesn't mean anything, Gram. I swear—"

"You don't have to swear nothing to me, honey." Gram coughed. "What do you say let's not make this any more of a shitty Christmas than it already is, huh?"

"Gram, please—I—"

"Good night."

"Maria? For heaven's sake." Nina was standing over me. The light in the apartment, bouncing off all that white, was blinding. My eyes burned from crying myself to sleep.

"There's a whole guest room. You didn't have to sleep here." Nina was already moving around the room. Arranging things, making notes, people to call, things to do.

"I know." I sat up. I still had the cordless phone in my hand.

"Is everything okay? Or is that a silly question?" Nina sat down next to me on the sofa. I shook my head no. She smoothed my hair. I started crying again.

"Oh, now." Nina put her arms around me.

"No, it's all ruined. Everything's ruined. Mom's right. It's all my fault."

"Shh, now. Whatever happened, I'm almost one hundred percent certain that it is *not* all your fault." Nina wiped a tear off my cheek.

"Yes, it is. I've been lying to everyone. I wasn't—I should've—" How could I even begin to explain this to Nina? To retrace my steps to where it all went haywire?

"Darling, listen to me. Your mother has a drug problem. You knew that much, didn't you?"

"I thought maybe . . ." I don't know what I thought. I knew I didn't want to think that my mother was on drugs.

"I apologize for putting you in the middle of our disagreement at the club the other day." Nina squeezed my hand. "You should know that she really has been trying. I helped her pay for an intensive rehabilitation facility last year, and it seemed that this might finally be the program that worked. I thought she might truly stay clean and sober. But even with the best intentions . . ." Nina trailed off.

"Is it because of me?" I asked. "I didn't realize . . . I was making it too stressful for her. With school and everything—I shouldn't have lied to her. I shouldn't have been so selfish—"

"Maria, stop it," Nina said firmly. "Your mother's actions have nothing to do with you. Victoria has struggled with her addiction for as long as I've known her. You have to know that she is enslaved to her demons, with or without your presence in her life. Frankly, after all these years, I'm starting to wonder why I bother. Or how it hasn't completely bankrupted me."

"Why do you bother?" I asked.

Nina folded her arms. "I'm afraid I have a terrible soft spot where your mother is concerned. It wasn't just her art. She was my friend. My marriage was falling apart, and, well—enter Victoria. With all her energy. When she was younger, she had a way of making everything an adventure. She had this thing about her that could light up a room. That may sound trite, but I don't know how to describe it any better. Your mother had this life, this joy, and it didn't matter that she didn't have money—" Nina stopped.

"Well, it mattered a little. I tried to help her as much as I could. I introduced her to everyone I knew in the art world, and she alienated them, one after another, with her behavior, or else stopped returning their calls when she realized they weren't offering a big payout up front. I gave her money, an apartment, a job. But it became so difficult. She was too erratic for the boutique. So I gave her Tony's job, managing Citygirls. That was an unequivocal disaster. I had her doing odd jobs for a while, but she went back to the drugs and her health issues became so drastic . . . Well, as you can see, she's better now. But it took some doing. After this last rehab, I gave her the coat check job. The simplest little thing, to ease her back in. And she still can't seem to show up. There's nothing left but custodial work, and I'm afraid she won't stoop to that. I thought moving her out to

Brooklyn, away from her usual scene, would help. But now it seems worse." Nina stood up and walked to her desk. I heard her light a cigarette.

"Was she ever a . . . dancer?"

"At the club?" Nina exhaled, laughing. "Heavens, no. Even if she'd wanted to. Your mother's about as coordinated as a dump truck."

"But she knows how to Pony," I murmured to myself.

"What's that?"

"Nothing."

"You don't mind if I smoke, do you?" Nina asked.

I shook my head.

"Maria, listen, you've got nothing to be embarrassed about, as far as your mother goes. She loves you very much, but she's your average, run-of-the-mill drug addict. It's a disease that is well out of her control. Out of anyone's control, really." Nina exhaled, a cloud of blue.

"What should we do now?"

"When it comes to Victoria, that's the million-dollar question, isn't it?" Nina waved her hand to clear the smoke from the air. "In the meantime, how about if I make you some breakfast?"

"No, thanks." The thought of food still made my throat close up.

"Coffee?" she said on her way to the kitchen.

"Okay."

The phone rang. I could hear water running.

"Just let the machine pick it up," Nina called out. After a few more rings, the machine clicked and beeped, and my mother's voice filled the apartment.

"Nina? Nina, are you there? This is Vic. I need you, Nina—I

really fucked up this time. I told Maria to leave yesterday, and—on Christmas—and she didn't come home last night." Her voice broke. I stood up. I didn't feel like hearing her voice. But I found myself walking toward the machine, like it was pulling me along. *I could just pick up the phone.*

"And I thought maybe she would have called you or maybe she's staying at your place. Maria, if you're listening, honey, it's Mom, and I'm so sorry. I'm so, so sorry. I just totally lost my shit, you know? And, um, I really hope you'll forgive me and everything will be okay again because, um. I'm just . . . I know, I'm a jerk. I'm a total shithead, I know I am. But I'm trying, I'm really— I'm gonna try harder, and I'm just so sorry for all the shitty things I said to you, Maria. I didn't mean it, I didn't mean any of it. Come home, okay? Will you? I love you, Maria. I'm sorry."

I stood by Nina's desk, frozen. Listening to the tape in the machine click and whirr.

"Hmm." Nina stood in the kitchen doorway, an empty coffee cup in her hand. "Sounds like that call was for you, anyway."

15

It took me a frightened second to recognize the bald guy in the trench coat who grabbed me by the shoulders as soon as I rounded the corner of Nina's street.

"Maria! Thank God! You're alive!" It was Lee. He hugged me, then looked me up and down. "Your hair looks fantastic."

"Thanks. Meanwhile, I'm having a mild heart attack."

"I'm sorry!" He took his hands off me. "But I couldn't help myself! Your mother's had me and the boy toy combing the streets—"

"The boy toy?"

"Oh, what's his name? Travis?"

"Travis," I repeated.

"Oh my God." Lee rolled his eyes. "He's going to get himself arrested. He's basically stalking the entire NYU campus, because he's obsessed with some obese pianist he's convinced you've eloped with."

"Tell Travis to go fuck himself," I muttered, walking away.

"Ooh, can I?" Lee caught up to me. "Listen, Maria, you have to call your mother. Tell her you haven't been chopped up into a million pieces and thrown into the Hudson River. Travis has her convinced that this guy you've been seeing is essentially the Son of Sam."

"You tell her."

"Tell her what? That I spotted you walking down Lexington Avenue in a fabulous plaid ensemble and you waved from a distance? Maria, your mother wants me to throw you over my shoulder and bring you home. Now, obviously, I'm not going to do that, because I'd put my back out, but—"

"I'm not going home."

"Where are you going, then?"

"I'm running an errand. I have to buy—" I consulted the list Nina had given me. "Beluga caviar."

"I knew it!" Lee gasped. "You've been kidnapped by that awful Nina woman, haven't you?"

"She's not awful." I moved to the edge of the sidewalk to let a dog walker with a bunch of tiny, yapping terriers pass by. "And I haven't been kidnapped. Mom told me to leave, so I left."

"Maria." Lee sighed. "I know how your mother can be. She has her ups and downs, and she has her little outbursts. But beneath it all, she's the same old Vic, and I know she loves you."

"She's got a funny way of showing it."

"I know." Lee reached into his pocket, pulled out a cell phone, and flipped it open. "Listen, if I can't convince you to come home, will you at least talk to her?"

"No."

"I'm dialing the number."

"Good for you." I turned and walked away. Lee followed.

"Here! It's ringing!" He held the phone out to me.

I swatted him away. "I'm not talking to her."

From the phone, I heard a tiny "Hello?" Lee pressed the phone to his ear.

"Vic! It's Lee! I found Maria! She's right here, but she doesn't want to talk to you." He put his hand over the receiver. "Talk to her!" he commanded.

I shook my head.

He got back on the phone. "Vic? Okay, she's in a bad mood, and she's shopping for Beluga caviar, which means that she's probably been hanging around Nina, but other than that, she's fine. And she says she'll talk to you soon. Yes . . . yes, I'll tell her. I think she already knows, but I'll tell her . . . Love you, too, babe. Ciao." He flipped the phone closed. "She wants me to tell you that she's so, so, so, so sorry—that's four 'so's. And will you please come home."

I shook my head. "Maybe later. But not right now." I jammed my hands farther into my pockets. "Tell her . . . tell her we'll talk soon, though."

"How soon?"

I shrugged. I was still angry. And I really wasn't sure when I'd feel like talking to my mom again.

"Maybe next year."

Nina's New Year's Eve party was going to be a serious shindig. She'd hired a chamber music group and caterers and everything. Almost a hundred people had been invited to come and watch the fireworks from her wraparound windows. I didn't know how a hundred people were going to fit in the apartment.

"You've been such a help, Maria. I don't know how I would've gotten this together without you." Nina and I were unwrapping crystal vases from their stowed-away place in the hall closet. She'd ordered a small mountain of fresh-cut flowers for the affair.

"I've been having a really good time," I told her. "And it's been really nice of you to let me stay here. But—"

"No buts about it. It's been wonderful having you." She crumpled a wad of newspaper in her hand.

"I know I should go back, though."

"No, you shouldn't. Here." She handed me a vase. "Put that one on the hall table. I think it'll be perfect for the gladiolas."

I obeyed.

"I mean, after the holiday, I was thinking I should maybe go back—I should go to the regular school. The public school in Brooklyn."

"Why?" Nina looked up. "I thought you enjoyed our lessons."

"I do. But I kind of feel like I'm in your hair. And, also . . . I was sorta thinking that maybe I could go to work for you."

"What do you mean, work for me?" Nina squinted into a crystal bowl, holding it up to the light, looking for cracks.

"I was thinking." I cleared my throat. "Maybe we could work out a deal. Maybe you could pay for my mom to go to rehab again, and I could take over her job at Citygirls. To pay it off."

"Maria." She looked down at me. "Don't be ridiculous. How would I explain that to your grandmother?"

"You wouldn't have to. We could say I'm working at the boutique—"

"My dear, little white lies are unbecoming, both to your mother and to you. Now, let's stop with this nonsense and finish the task at hand. What do you say?"

"I just thought it might work, that's all."

"And you'll live in the apartment by yourself? Or will you take over your mother's latest boyfriend, as well?" Nina arched her expertly plucked eyebrow at me. I felt myself blush.

"No," I muttered.

"You'll live here, we'll continue our lessons, and that's that." Nina handed me the crystal bowl. It was heavier than I thought. "I think your grandmother would prefer it, don't you?"

"Yeah." I looked down at the bowl, the light prisming off of it. "Yes, ma'am. I guess she would."

My feet were killing me. I ducked into the kitchen to hide out for a while and kick off the heels I'd borrowed from Nina. The party was even worse than one of Grandmother's Thanksgiving dinners. Everybody was old and boring and rich, and there really were almost a hundred of them. My cheeks hurt from fake-smiling. And I'd had no idea that I'd signed on as the hired help. I was put in charge of piling up the coats on the bed in the spare room—my room—and helping the bartender make sure the glasses stayed full. And letting the caterers know which trays were empty. I hadn't even gotten anything to eat yet. I couldn't help looking out Nina's windows and imagining my mom out there, downtown, somewhere in the crowd at the Patti Smith show. I wondered if it was too late for me to get in.

In the quiet of the kitchen, I stole a flute of champagne and swiped a few miniquiches from one of the caterer's trays. I was only alone for a moment, though, before the kitchen door swung open and two women came in, both of them giggling drunkenly.

"Ooh, we didn't know anybody else was in here!" One of them clamped her hand over her mouth, still giggling.

"Is it okay if we smoke?"

My mouth was stuffed with miniquiches, so I just nodded.

"Thank God." The taller one with the frosted tips lit up. "Smoke?" She offered one to me.

I swallowed. "No, thanks."

"If you haven't started yet, then don't," the shorter one with the obvious facelift advised. "I'm sorry, tell me your name again. I know Nina introduced us."

"Maria."

"Right, right." The woman with the facelift nodded. "I'm Jaclyn, and this is Edith."

"We met." Edith exhaled smoke at me. "So, you work for the caterers? Those sushi things are fabulous."

"No, I'm—I'm a friend of Nina's."

"She's Veronica's daughter, remember?" Jaclyn elbowed Edith.

"Who's Veronica?"

"Victoria," I corrected.

"You know. Remember when Carl had that affair with Holzberg's wife and they split up for a while?"

"Oh God. When Nina wrecked the Porsche?"

"Mm-hmm. But not before that incident in the Hamptons—"

"I remember that. She went to Holzberg's and threw that painting in the pool—wasn't it a Schnabel?"

"Ucch," Jaclyn gave a throaty sigh. "I can't keep those new painters straight. Anyway, you remember, she took up with that sort of . . . new waver. Running around downtown—"

"I thought she was dead. The girl who worked at Nina's boutique? That's the same one, right? I heard she collapsed right there in the store. Massive heart attack. Nina was the one who did CPR until the paramedics arrived. I think it was drug related. She wasn't that old."

"I think you must have the wrong—" I started to say.

"Is that what happened?" Jaclyn sucked on her cigarette. "You poor thing. Your mother died, and now you live here with Nina?"

"My mother's not—"

"Lucky you." Edith snorted. "If you're gonna jump class, might as well get adopted into it, instead of having to marry some bastard like my husband."

"Christ. Don't get me started." Jaclyn rolled her eyes.

"Would you excuse me, please?" I walked out, barefoot, forgetting my shoes. Nina's shoes. She had everyone gathered at the windows. Dressed in shiny pink and green cardboard hats. One of the caterers was distributing noisemakers on a silver tray.

"Maria, there you are!" Nina waved me over. "It's almost time!" There was a tiny television set on her desk. Dick Clark was on, counting down the last two minutes of the year. I shook my head and headed for the bedroom. She wedged her way through the clusters of drunk old rich people and caught up to me in the hallway.

"Maria—where are your shoes?"

"In the kitchen."

"Come, now, let's not be—"

"Have you been telling people that my mother's dead?"

"What?"

"These women—Edith and Janice, or something—they said—"

"Why would you listen to a word either of those women—"

"They said she had a heart attack. Why would they say something like that? Is it true? Why didn't anybody tell me?"

"Maria. Don't get hysterical." Nina sighed and pulled me into the spare bedroom, closing the door behind her. "There are some things that are simply too complicated—"

"Don't tell me I won't understand. I'm not some idiot who wandered in from—"

"From Millville, South Carolina. Thinking your wonderful mother hung the moon. Darling, it's not that you won't understand. It's that you'll understand all too well, and then you'll wish you didn't."

"Try me." I folded my arms across my chest.

"Maria." Nina's expression was blank. "Your mother is going to kill herself."

"That's a really . . . that's a really awful thing to say."

"Unfortunately, it's true. I told you that your mother was a drug addict. Last year, her heart finally gave out. Your mother was dead, as a matter of fact. Clinically dead, for a minute and a half. They brought her back, at the hospital. And the doctors told her that if she ever abuses drugs again, she will effectively end her life within one to two years. You would think"—Nina cleared her throat—"that being clinically dead would be a strong deterrent to bad behavior. For Victoria, unfortunately, it isn't."

"Why didn't—why didn't anybody tell me she was sick?"

"Because everyone wants you to do well. No one wants you wasting your time worrying about someone who is already far beyond—she's beyond help, Maria. Beyond anything you or I could do. I've sent her to the best rehab facilities, to the best doctors. And she relapses, again and again. What else is left? Put her under twenty-four-hour surveillance? Admit her to the hospital? Throw her in jail?"

"But she's not—she's not sick. She could stop. She could be fine." Hot tears spilled out of my eyes. Outside, the countdown had started. The year was almost gone.

"Maria, you have to understand what I'm telling you." Nina put her hand on my shoulder. "Victoria doesn't think she's sick, either. But she is. And the one thing she cannot do is stop. Your mother was given an ultimatum: If you use drugs, you will die. No loopholes, no exceptions. Yet she continues. The equation cannot be any simpler."

"I don't buy it." I tossed Nina's hand off my shoulder. From the living room, an eruption of voices shouted *Happy New Year!*

"It doesn't matter whether or not you *buy* it. It's the truth."

"So, what, we just give up on her?" I heard my voice crack. "That's what you all want me to do? Wash my hands of her? Say, Sorry you're having trouble with drugs, Mom, but I have to think about my SATs."

"Yes, that's precisely what you're supposed to do. What has your mother ever given up for you? She left you because there weren't enough drugs in Millville to sustain her appetites. She threw you out of her apartment on Christmas Day because she was under the impression that you had gotten into her precious stash. Your mother has one love in her life; it isn't that ridiculous boyfriend of hers, and it isn't you. Maria, you have a chance. Your grandmother and I put you in a school that would have assured you a place on the top of college admissions lists. You cannot allow this to drag you down—"

"I *cannot allow this to drag me down?*"

"No, you cannot. And if it sounds heartless or cold, it's only because I've allowed it to drag me down for almost as long as you've been alive. I came to terms, only very recently, with the fact that I cannot be your mother's savior."

"And just because you've given up, you want me to give up, too?"

"I want you to save yourself. Do you have any idea how much it pains me to see how your mother abuses you?"

"She's never laid a hand—"

"She neglects you. She doesn't care about you. And it's unfortunate, because there are a lot of people on this planet who would love to have a daughter like you. A daughter who's smart and funny and curious about life. But your mother can't care about anything. She's already in thrall to this oblivion, to numbness and death. She's checking out of life, Maria, and she's going to end up in a very dark place, eventually in the darkest of places. And that's not your journey to make. You're at the dawn of your life. Don't let Victoria take you down with her."

A cold, sick chill had settled in my guts. Nina didn't know what she was talking about. Doctors weren't always right. Anyway, my mom didn't want to die. She was having too much fun.

"Even if you're right," I said, my voice thick with tears, "she's still my mother. I'm not giving up on her."

"Yes, she is still your mother. And no one can stop you from caring about her. But do you understand now? Do you understand why we kept this from you?"

"No. I think you're all fucked." I spat the words at her. "I think you're lying because you want me to hate her. You, my grandmother, my dad—"

"Your father, for what it's worth, had high hopes for your visit. After years of being somewhat at odds with his own mother, I think he would like to see you have a less fraught relationship with yours." Nina frowned. "As for me, if I truly wanted you to hate your mother, I would take you to the places she goes when she doesn't show up at work. If I wanted you to think ill of her, I would introduce you to some of the people she calls friends—"

"What about your friends? I guess it's okay for them to come to your house and drink tons of booze and talk shit about people, but you expect my mother to be some perfect saint. So what if she isn't? She's an artist."

"She was an artist, once."

"She still is! You think just because she didn't get rich and famous, you and your bitchy friends can sit around and cluck your tongues about what a tragedy she is. Well, guess what— she's not a tragedy. She's not somebody you have to save me from. You want me to come here and live with you and be some perfect little replicant. Well, I think that fucking sucks."

"Maria, turn around."

"What?"

"For heaven's sake, I'm not trying to turn you into a replicant. Turn around."

I turned.

"Do you see that painting?"

"Yes."

"Your mother painted it."

"I know that." It was huge, hanging over the bed. I could tell it was my mother's as soon as I saw it. The colors she used, the purples and blues. The way it was sort of abstract but you could see shapes, the way you can see shapes in clouds. The suggestion of an angel floating above a nighttime sea.

"If your mother had cared anything about herself, about her career, she could have easily sold that painting for thousands of dollars. Maybe even hundreds of thousands. But instead, she brought it to me. She was broke and strung out. She begged me to buy it from her, for the price of a fix. I finally agreed, thinking that, at the very least, I could safeguard her work until she was clean again. Would you like to know what I paid for your mother's painting, Maria?"

I shook my head. I didn't.

"Fifty-five dollars," Nina said quietly. "Cash."

Tears ran down my face. I couldn't stop them.

"Now you understand," Nina said. "And don't you wish you didn't?" She whipped a few Kleenex out of the box on the desk and handed them to me. "Here, clean up your face and come back to the party. Our guests will start to wonder."

I couldn't speak. I couldn't stop looking at my mother's painting. Suddenly, I saw everything in it. It was more like looking out of a window than into a painting. I saw the entire city reeling into the night. I saw the night the way my mother saw it. Shrouded, violent, and cursed. I saw my mother smoking cigarettes in the dark. I saw her in the light, how pale she was, how dark her eyes. I saw that I wasn't going to win. Nina wasn't going to win, either. My mother was going to be the only survivor. My mother was going to live forever, in the blacks and blues of this painting.

Outside, fireworks boomed in the sky like thunder. The entire living room sang "Auld Lang Syne." Nina put her hand on my shoulder, then let it drop. She left, closing the door behind her. I blew my nose, wiped my face, wiped my hands on my dress. Nina's dress. My hands trembled at the zipper, shook as I pulled off the silk stockings and the lacy push-up bra. I opened the closet and pulled out my old black sweatshirt and my baggy jeans. I put on heavy socks, laced up my boots. Jammed everything else into my backpack. I was leaving.

In the living room, everyone was watching the fireworks. No one stopped me. I just walked out.

I ran down the sidewalk, not sure where I was going. Just running. The cold air seemed to split my lungs. The sidewalks were crowded with people in party hats who peered out of the double nines in plastic eyeglasses shaped like the new year. They blew horns and kazoos and popped tiny confetti champagne bottles. The streets were flooded with people—the entire crowd, the thousands that had filled Times Square to watch the ball drop, was dissipating. All those crazy, freezing people were making their way back uptown and down, to their apartments and hotels. I ran to the corner of the park, to the Plaza Hotel and the horse-drawn carriages, into the train station to catch the N downtown.

* * *

By the time I found the Bowery Ballroom, the doors were locked and there was no one around but the stage crew, dressed in black, with Mardi Gras beads around their necks, as they loaded big black cases of sound equipment into a truck. I looked in the windows of all the diners nearby, searching for Mom. But there was no sign of her. I walked uptown, then west. Toward the water. Past the Chelsea Hotel.

Lee's door was propped open, the elevator waiting. I pressed the button for his loft and listened to the rusty gears grinding. I was met at the top by a bare-chested guy with ripped muscles wearing only a diaper, a pair of Doc Martens, and a sash that read, in glitter, OH BABY NEW YEAR!

"Can I help you?" He gave me a kind smile.

"Is Lee here?"

"He's over at the bar—come on in."

Lee's loft was completely transformed. A DJ in the corner spun trance music, and red lights swung around in the darkness. The room was packed with men—tall, short, old, young, some in costume, all of them drinking, dancing with each other, throwing confetti, laughing. The only women there were so made-up and androgynous looking, they had to be either drag queens or supermodels.

"Maria!" Lee saw me before I recognized him. He was wearing a long silver robe, a fake gray beard, and a sash that matched the one on the guy at the front door. Lee's read: YOU ARE SO LAST YEAR!

"Lee, have you seen my mom?"

"No, honey—she's doing her Patti Smith thing."

"I know. I tried to find her, but—"

"What? Come over here. I can't hear you."

I followed Lee to his bedroom, behind the Chinese screens. It wasn't much quieter. He pulled off the silly fake beard. "You look like hell, kid." He wiped a mascara smudge off my cheek. "What's going on?"

I shook my head. I didn't have the energy to tell him the whole story.

"I just need to see her. I need to—there's so much I have to say."

"Okay, don't get upset. We'll find her. How about if I get you a drink? A little wine?"

Yeah. Get me drunk. That's the answer.

"No, thanks."

"Ginger ale, then? Hang on—stay right there, okay?"

I wandered over to the window. I could see the lights of the city and my reflection all at once. The river running into my own face, the lights of the buildings and the cars tracing the outlines of my hair. I wished I could really become all of it somehow. Or that it could become a part of me. That I could have those lights inside me. That movement. All that aliveness. Because at that moment, all I felt was afraid. And the fear tightened my guts and my throat. The fear made me feel like I was hardening inside. Like I was turning to stone.

"It's beautiful, isn't it?" Lee handed me a glass. He lit a cigarette. "It's a beautiful city."

"I don't know." My hand slipped on the glass. I tightened my grip. "Maybe it's a beast. Maybe it just eats people alive. Maybe that's the way it lives."

"Kid, don't go getting all dramatic on me." Lee smiled. "You're gonna be fine. Your mom's gonna be fine. You'll talk it out, you'll cry, you'll laugh, you'll do each other's hair. Trust me."

I watched him take a drag off his cigarette.

"You mind if I bum one of those?"

"Tsk." Lee looked up at me. "And stunt your growth?"

I walked east until I found myself in front of Gram's dorm. I didn't bother to call first to see if he was there. I didn't even bother to wait on the elevator. I ran up the stairs, taking two at a time. Out of breath, I pounded on the door. He had to be home. If he wasn't, I would wait.

"Hey." It was Sandy, Gram's roommate. "Maria, right?"

"Uh-huh. Is Gram here?" I was still gasping for air.

"Um, hang on, okay?" Sandy closed the door and left me standing out in the hall. I swallowed hard and tried to smooth down my hair. After a few minutes, the door opened again.

"Gram—"

"Hey." He stood there with one hand on the door, a flat black box tucked under his other arm.

"I really need your help—" I stepped toward him. He backed away.

"I hate to hear that," he said. "You know, this whole thing's been pretty humiliating. I'd rather you not come back here again."

"Please, Gram. I just need to talk to you—"

"I don't think that's a good idea." He handed me the box. "Here. Take this. I can't listen to it anymore." I realized what it was. The George Harrison album. *All Things Must Pass.* Gram started to close the door. I stuck my heavy boot in its way.

"Wait!" We were just inches apart now. He backed away again. "I have to tell you this. I wouldn't have spent the night with you if I didn't really care about you. I wanted to tell you, but I got scared. I was afraid you wouldn't—" He wasn't even looking at me. He was looking out over my head, his eyes full of tears. "I know how bad it is. What I did to you. I know how bad it feels to be lied to. And I'm sorry. I just need you to know that I'm not . . . I'm not what you think I am."

He finally looked at me. "I don't have the faintest idea what you are."

16

Downstairs, at Citygirls, the music was thumping. I stood on the corner, looking up at the apartment. There was a light on in what used to be my room. The living room. Someone was home.

I went upstairs and unlocked the door. The place was a mess. Dishes stacked in the sink. Take-out containers piled by the trash. I could hear softly plucked guitars coming from the stereo, and, on top of it, another guitar there in the room. Travis sat on the end of the pulled-out futon, strumming his guitar along with the record player Mom gave me for Christmas. I didn't recognize the song, but it sounded almost like a hymn. The singer kept singing *Jesus, help me find my proper place.*

"Hey," I called out.

He didn't look up. "I thought it might be you." He stopped plucking his guitar. "I don't know why. I didn't have any reason to think it would be. But here you are. The prodigal daughter returns."

"I'm not prodigal. Mom asked me to leave."

"Whatever."

"Where is she?"

"Still at the Patti show with her friends."

"You didn't go?"

"I got uninvited." He strummed the guitar. "There's a card for you on the kitchen table. It came in the mail a couple of days ago. From your dad."

I found the green envelope with my name on it and slit it open. It was a Christmas card, with a cartoon Santa stuck in a chimney and a joke caption that wasn't funny. When I opened the card, something fell out. I picked it up off the floor. It was a Polaroid snapshot of a motor scooter, parked in our driveway at home. Beneath it, in my father's crooked scrawl, it said "Merry Christmas, Slugger."

It took me a minute to make sense of it. Then I remembered. Thanksgiving. Out on the porch at Grandmother's. Of all the things he could've picked to remember.

"I was kidding about the motorcycle," I said to no one.

"What?" Travis said.

"Nothing." I stuffed the picture back in the envelope.

"So, where've you been lately?" Travis asked. He put down his guitar and walked over to the kitchen table.

"With Nina." I gritted my teeth, remembering how angry I was with him. "Why didn't you tell me Mom was sick? Why didn't you tell me she had a heart attack last year?"

"There's a lot of stuff I wasn't supposed to tell you." He didn't look up.

"Yeah, that's everybody's favorite game these days, isn't it?

Don't Tell Maria." I crossed my arms. "Why'd you tell Gram to stay away from me?"

"I didn't tell him to stay away from you."

"Well, he doesn't want to see me anymore, so if you're out to ruin my life, mission accomplished."

"I told him to be careful with you."

"I wish you hadn't told him anything at all." I felt like I was going to cry again, but I'd been crying so much lately, I didn't have any tears left. "He's the only friend I had up here."

"What about me?"

"What about you? You're my mother's boyfriend."

"Yeah. I guess that's what I am," he said. I suddenly realized how close he was standing.

"Travis." I took a small step away from him. "Why did you kiss me that day?" He hesitated, scratching his beard stubble with the back of his hand.

"I don't know. I just felt like—I dunno. Something came over me. Ever since you got here, I . . ." He frowned. "I was thinking about leaving her, you know. Before you came."

"You stayed because of me?"

He shrugged.

"That's crazy," I whispered, barely able to talk.

"Don't you think—" He licked his cracked lips. "Do you think maybe we could try—" He touched my cheek. I closed my eyes and opened them again. He was still Travis. The top buttons of his shirt were undone. I touched the tattoo over his heart.

"Who's Aileen, anyway?" I asked him.

"My mom."

I closed my eyes again. He rested his hand on my neck. I

could feel him moving closer to me. I could smell the sweetness of his breath.

"Travis, don't."

He stopped. His hand dropped.

"Christ. You're right. It's crazy, isn't it?" He exhaled. "You're lucky, Maria. You're too smart to fuck up like this."

No, I wanted to tell him. *I'm not smart at all. Everybody keeps insisting that I'm so smart, but I keep acting so stupid.*

"I'm sorry, kid." Travis kissed the top of my head. "I'm sorry you had to get dragged down into all this crap between me and your mom. I'm just sorry as hell." He looked hard at me, and I thought he was going to cry, himself.

"Don't worry about it."

Travis shook his head. He closed his eyes tight, pressing his thumbs deep into his sockets. Then he patted me on the head and walked back into the bathroom. I'd had my backpack on my back the entire time. I was so exhausted, I hadn't even realized I was still carrying it. I dropped it on the floor, the edges strained square with the record box Gram had given me. Forget it; I'd unpack in the morning. I lay down on the futon and closed my eyes. In the seconds before I fell asleep, I heard Travis turning the bathroom faucet on, then off. The record ended. I heard the metal clink of Travis's belt sliding off.

I don't know how long I slept, if I slept at all, before I heard the crash. The scattering of broken glass. I jerked awake and stood up. The bathroom door was still closed. I walked over. I didn't hear a sound.

"Travis?" I knocked. No answer. "Travis, are you okay in there?" I knocked again. "Travis, you're kinda freaking me out. Is everything okay?" I turned the knob. It was unlocked. But when I pushed on the door, there was something heavy pressing against it. *Travis.*

I threw my entire body against the door. When I finally wedged it open, I saw Travis in a heap on the tiles. His belt was tied around his arm. There was a needle sticking out of the crook of his elbow. I yanked it out and his blood spurted, drops of it hitting my face. I thought I might be sick. There was blood everywhere. Somehow, when he collapsed, he'd pulled the medicine cabinet down off the wall. There were pills and Band-Aids and broken glass everywhere. And all this blood. His hands were cut. I pressed my head to his heart. I could hear his heartbeat, and he was still breathing. I wasn't sure whether to try CPR or what. I ran out to the phone and dialed 911.

"911, what's your emergency?"

"My friend— He's had a— He's overdosing on drugs—"

"Calm down, miss. What's your address?"

"You have to send help—"

"We will, miss, but I need to know where you are."

"If you could just tell me what to do." I stretched the phone cord into the bathroom and knelt next to Travis. He was still breathing. Still breathing. "I just need to know what to do."

"Miss, please calm down. We need you to tell us where you are."

"I'm in Brooklyn. I'm—" God, I couldn't even remember the address. "By the BQE. The apartment above Citygirls."

The sun was already up when the doctor came out to the waiting room and told me that Travis was going to be all right. When he told me, I sort of collapsed a little, and they tried to make me stay. They shone a light in my eyes, but I told them that I wasn't the one on drugs. I told them I had to find my mother, and when the nurse was out of the room, I left.

I found a pay phone near the hospital and called the apartment. When I walked back, I saw the place where the wooden doorjamb had been shredded when they rushed Travis out on the stretcher. The bathroom was still a wreck, the broken glass and plaster still in the sink. Mom wasn't there. I wrote a quick note and left it on the table. *Mom—Travis at hospital on Atlantic.* No drawings. I grabbed my backpack and took the subway into Manhattan. It took a minute for me to realize why everyone was staring at me. Then I looked down and saw the dried blood on the collar of the white undershirt I wore beneath my sweatshirt. I felt my face and realized the blood had dried there, too, hardened into tiny scabs. I flicked them off and adjusted my sweatshirt. The train lurched and sped.

I reached into the front pocket of my backpack and took out my Walkman. I kept at least four Supergirl Mixtapes with me at all times, so that no matter what mood I was in, I would have something to listen to. But suddenly there was nothing, no music that I wanted to hear. I searched the cassette boxes, the song titles blurring together in front of my eyes. None of this was going to help. I put on my headphones, but I didn't push play. The whine and groan of the train wheels got a little quieter. That was all.

St. Mark's Church was somewhere downtown, I knew that much. I remembered Mom pointing it out when we were walking somewhere, maybe the time we went to the movies. Or maybe it was when we bought all those clothes. I walked and walked, thinking I might recognize where I was. Wishing I hadn't left behind the Manhattan diary that Nina gave me, the one with all the maps. Finally, I stopped enough people on the street until I found someone who knew where I was going. He pointed me in the right direction, but when I got there, the doors were locked. According to the sign, the all-day reading didn't start for another two hours.

I didn't feel like I could walk another step, but I did. I walked, losing track of the blocks, until I came to another church. A real church. The doors were wide open. I walked in and crossed myself. Sat down in a back pew. I knelt down to pray, but I started crying again instead. The only words I could think of were "Forgive me, Father, for I have sinned." But I couldn't remember the rest. I sat back in the pew and fell asleep.

It seemed like only a few minutes later that someone was shaking me back to consciousness.

"Wake up, dear." I bolted upright. There was an elderly priest standing over me. "I didn't mean to frighten you. I only wanted to tell you that we have a shelter, if you've nowhere else to go."

"No, I'm sorry, I just fell asleep. What time is it?"

"It's half past four."

"Oh, no." I grabbed my backpack.

"Are you sure I can't help you, miss?"

"No, Father, but thank you." I ran out into the street. The streetlamps were on. It was dusk. I'd slept almost the entire day.

The all-day reading was going on into the night, but my mom wasn't there. I didn't have enough for the admission, but the door guy let me in to look for her. I came back outside and found a place against the low stone wall to sit and lean and wait. I found an open side door where I could sneak in and out every once in a while to use the bathroom. It was the only reason to leave my post, besides going to the pay phone to call the apartment every hour. I got Lee's number from 411 and tried calling there, too. No one picked up but the machines.

It was almost ten o'clock and it was freezing outside. I ran to the deli down the block for a hot chocolate and tried the apartment again. Still no answer, and I was down to the last of my change. I hugged my jacket around me and shivered. Leaned back against my clothes-stuffed backpack, but it was hard and uncomfortable. Then I remembered—I still had that stupid record in there. The George Harrison one, from Gram.

I unzipped my backpack and took the record out. I held it flat in my lap. Leaned back against the bag and closed my eyes to rest for a moment. A gust of wind caught the edge of the album cover and flapped it open. I snapped awake. The wind made my eyes tear. But when I went to close the album cover, I saw something I hadn't noticed before. Faint green letters, tiny, slanting across the inside of the box.

For Victoria. With all my loving. Al.

I closed the cover and wiped my eyes. That poor sap. My dad.

"Hey."

I looked up, thinking it was my mom. My eyes blurred again. Another woman stood over me, wearing a black wool cap and jacket. The man beside her wore an old fedora and carried a guitar. They looked like gypsies. Both of them with their hair in their eyes.

"That's a great album," she said.

"Yeah. I know."

She kind of nodded at me and smiled, then reached down

and dropped a quarter into my near-empty hot chocolate cup. I fished it out, wiping the chocolate off on the leg of my jeans. I looked down at the album cover, at George alive among those jolly, grinning gnomes. Those fake, frozen gnomes. And George, alive and sad and real. I traced his faded gray hat with my cold fingers.

"Oh my God!"

I jumped, looking up. Another woman I'd never seen before bent down, her alarmed face close to mine. "Was that her?"

"Who?"

"Was that Patti? Patti Smith? Wasn't that her, talking to you just now?" The woman looked almost angry. "What did she say to you?"

"I—uh—"

"Rachel, hurry up! Get the camera! I think I just saw Patti!" Another girl caught up to the first one, and they ran after the woman in the black cap, toward the church. I looked down at the quarter in my hand. Stood up, my legs stiff and aching. I packed the record back into my bag. I was going to make one last call.

"Maria!"

Finally, my mother.

"You made it!" She threw her arms around me. "I'm so sorry."

"I know." My voice was muffled in her hair. I was so glad to see her. I wanted to keep holding on to her, to keep her close to me. But she pulled away and looked at me, her eyes full of tears.

"Hey. I knew you'd forgive me," she whispered.

I shrugged and tried to smile.

"I want you to meet some people. You remember Paula, from Travis's show at CBs. And this is Kelly, Andrea, and Maureen. They're all friends of mine from the Patti shows. Guys, this is Maria." They said their hellos. I didn't say anything. She sent them on ahead to find seats.

"Is everything— Are you okay?"

"I'm great! The show was amazing. I was just so unhappy thinking you were mad at me. I'm so glad you're here now!"

"I mean—do you . . . feel okay?"

"I'm great." She put her hand on her hip and gave me a knowing look. "Come on, kiddo. You don't have to worry about me. Just a momentary freak-out. You know how those are."

"Yeah." I bit my lip. "So you haven't been home yet? Since last night?"

"No. Honey, what's wrong? You look like a ghost."

Like you've *seen* a ghost, I started to correct her. But then I realized that I probably did.

"It's, uh—" Where should I begin? *It's everything. It's Travis. It's Nina. It's me. It's you.*

But she didn't know anything. She was still innocent. And all of a sudden, I understood. I understood why my dad didn't want me coming up here. Why everybody wanted to keep their secrets to themselves. It was nice to be innocent. To not know. It was peaceful. It was good.

"It's Travis," I told her. "He's fine now, but he's in the hospital."

"Oh my God—what happened?"

"He OD'd last night."

"What?" She clapped her hand over her mouth.

"They took him to the hospital near us. They said he's going to be okay. But he's still there."

"Oh my God." She shook her head and looked up at the sky. "Oh my God," she repeated.

"Vic, everything okay?" One of her friends, Maureen, was back at the gate.

"Everything's fine." Mom put on a broad smile.

"Hurry up, willya? We got great seats, and Patti's gonna read soon."

"I'll be right there."

Maureen went back inside. Mom was still shaking her head, muttering. "Travis, you idiot." She bit her fingernail and looked up at me. "He knows better. He was trying to quit. That's the junkie mistake, you know? You try to quit, and your body forgets what it's like. Your resistance is gone. Then you try to take the dose you used to take, and . . . *pfft*."

And pfft?

"I guess you would know," I said. She looked at me. I looked back at her. No more joking around.

"Maria." She rolled her eyes. "*Maria.*" She threw up her hands. "Okay. What do you want me to say? Because I don't even know where to start."

"You should probably start with Travis." I slung my backpack over my shoulder. Mom glanced back toward St. Mark's, toward the warm orange lights in the doorway. "But you're actually thinking about staying here with your friends, aren't you?"

She kept looking at the church, then back at me.

"You think Patti Smith gives a shit if you're there in that audience tonight?" My voice came out sharp.

"What?"

"Because Travis needs—" I exhaled. She was blinking back tears. I softened my voice. "Travis needs somebody to take care of him."

"I know he does." She nodded. Her voice was small. "I just don't know if that person should be me."

I took her face in my hands and kissed her on the forehead. Then I hugged her tight. I probably looked like a little kid, but I didn't care. I pressed my ear to her chest, right below her collarbone. I could hear her heart thudding its rhythm. She seemed fine. *She was going to be fine.*

"Hey, kiddo . . ." My mother patted my head.

I pulled away from her. "I'll see you later."

"Where are you going?" she called after me.

"Just going off by myself for a while."

I didn't have to walk very far. I found my phone booth and shut myself inside. Jammed my quarter into the slot and dialed. The voice on the other end of the line asked for more quarters. I consulted the secret pocket in my bag and found enough to oblige. The phone rang. I prayed that I was right. That he'd taken today off to watch football, at least.

"Hello?"

"Dad?"

"Maria?"

"Yeah, it's me."

"Well, happy new year, honey. How's everything up there in the big city?"

"Oh, it's uh—" I sniffed. But I was done crying. For now, anyway. "It's been better."

"Sugar pie? Are you okay?"

"I'm fine, Dad. I was just wondering if we could talk a little."
There was a lot I wanted to ask him. A lot I wanted to say.

"Sure, let me just turn this ball game off."

"Would you just promise me one thing, though?"

"Anything you want."

"Just . . . promise me you won't say 'I told you so.'"

ACKNOWLEDGMENTS

Not to get all country music on you guys, but first things first: I want to thank the fans—yes, that means you. Thanks for reading, thanks for coming to the readings, thanks for the positive Internet messages, and thanks for frequenting your local libraries and bookstores. On that note, I'd like to thank the Ocean Township Library and the Asbury Park Public Library for the free writing space and reading materials, respectively. Thank you to the staff, nurses, doctors, and management, past and present, at New Jersey Urologic Institute (formerly Shore Urology) for being cool about the time off I took to finish this thing. Thank you, Jackie Sheeler, for the trip to Seattle, and thanks to Michele Angelo for appreciating the finer points of both Gram Parsons and Johnny Thunders. Thanks to Tony Sabo for being a cooler drummer than the one in this book. Extra gratitude to Heather, Liz, Hannah, and Flip for nearly twenty years (twenty years!) of being the Support Team. Thank you to Ryan for sharing your love of Bone Thugs and Jim Nabors, and to Mike and Wendy, who are still showing up. Thanks to Dr. Brown's 100-sentence grammar exam, to Lee Vasbinder for the typing lessons, and to

Margaret Sullivan Howie and Jo Woodyard for years of support. Biggest thanks to my family in the Southern states, who put up with a lot of shenanigans but keep inviting me back for the holidays anyway. Extra thanks to my grandmas, my brother Chris, and my mom, who gave me most of her best records and who bought me a copy of *Horses* when I was sixteen, not to mention *Led Zeppelin IV* back in junior high. Apologies in advance to Manya for the "salt and pepper." Thanks to Emily and Kate for hanging in there with me. And most of all, thanks to Jeff for suffering the early drafts, and for bringing it all back home.